Louisa Jane Hall

The Sheaves of Love

A fireside story

Louisa Jane Hall

The Sheaves of Love
A fireside story

ISBN/EAN: 9783744748629

Printed in Europe, USA, Canada, Australia, Japan

Cover: Foto ©Andreas Hilbeck / pixelio.de

More available books at **www.hansebooks.com**

THE

SHEAVES OF LOVE.

A Fireside Story.

"There is that maketh himself rich, yet hath nothing; there is that maketh himself
poor, yet hath great riches."—SOLOMON.

BOSTON:

PUBLISHED BY L. J. PRATT.

1861.

BOSTON:

DAMRELL AND MOORE, PRINTERS AND BOOKBINDERS,

16 Devonshire Street.

TO THE

YOUTH OF OUR BELOVED COUNTRY,

THIS BOOK

𝔜𝔰 𝔇𝔢𝔡𝔦𝔠𝔞𝔱𝔢𝔡.

CONTENTS.

THE SHEAVES OF LOVE.

CHAPTER I.

A DISCARDED PLAN.

" WHAT now, my fair cousin!" exclaimed Fred
Whiting, as in no very gentlemanly manner he
rushed into his father's library. "I say, Alice, I
had no idea of finding you here. I thought women's time was all taken up with that endless embroidery and fancy work, though I never could see
any use or propriety in it. But, as I was going to
say, I thought father's library contained no works of
fiction. Why, bless me!"—and Fred's eyes grew
larger and brighter as he read—"'Book of Entertaining Knowledge.' Well, I declare, Alice,"
he exclaimed, "if you aren't a perfect puzzle!
Why I never, in my wildest moments, supposed
that woman's intellect was capable of grasping any
thing higher than fiction. Pray, what do you read
it for?"

Cousin Fred stopped a moment to take breath;
for these questions and observations had been poured

1

forth in a much less time than it has taken us to
record them. And, while Alice is trying to frame
an answer for them all, we also will ask one question. Who was Frederick Whiting?

Frederick Whiting was the only son of William
Whiting, Esq., a wealthy merchant of New York.
He was one of the favored, or rather unfortunate,
children of wealth ; for his father's money and influence, while it had procured him every advantage of
society and education, had also surrounded him with
a crowd of flatterers, who filled his mind with ideas
of his own personal importance and superiority.

Yet Fred Whiting, despite his faults, had an
unselfish, affectionate disposition, which a happy
home and judicious training would have strengthened, and which, under proper influences, would
have rendered him a character estimable for all
good and moral qualities. But he found little sympathy in his family. All had different tastes, and he
sought elsewhere that society and enjoyment which
his own home should have afforded.

He was now seventeen years of age, and for two
years had been attending school, with a view to
enter college. He was at home, spending his vacation ; and with the boyish, fun-loving spirit of his
age, he had teased his mother, hectored his sisters,
and bothered the servants to the last point of endur-
ance, and, as his mother said, " pestered the whole
household generally." Of his cousin, who was of

a quiet, studious temperament, he had taken but little notice, save to rally her upon her "dark brown studies," as he called them. But, upon the morning in question, he had exhausted his ingenuity in expedients for fun and frolic-making. It was a foggy, rainy morning in November; and his elder sister had not yet arisen, knowing she should have no callers in that weather; his mother had taken refuge in her room, under a severe fit of headache and of *ennui;* and his younger sister, of the age of Alice, was visiting for the day at a young friend's. He had repaired to the kitchen: but John, the coachman, had gone away some miles upon business; and the cook, a faithful old sable, who had served the family for many years, said she "done wish young massa 'd cl'ar out, and leab de kitchen to honest folks as minded der own 'fairs."

In this dilemma he suddenly bethought himself of Alice. "I'll hunt her up," thought he. But no Alice was to be found. Every imaginable place was ransacked; dark holes and corners received the benefit of his bright, prying eyes. And even clothes-rooms and china-closets were opened, with no success; for Fred would as soon have thought of looking into the stables for one of the family, as into his father's library.

It was a grand old room, with heavy oaken wainscots and panellings; and its bay windows were shaded with rich crimson curtains.

As Fred impulsively threw open the door, he
started back as if half ashamed of intruding.   There
sat Alice, her head resting upon her hand, and the
traces of tears still upon her cheeks.   It was evident that she had not expected to be disturbed, for
her book had slipped from her hand, and now rested
upon her lap.   But she rose with a smile, and
seemed anxious to conceal her recent agitation.

It was wholly unnecessary; for Fred had eyes
for nothing but fun.   He picked up the book; and
a glance at the title-page had so astonished him, as
to give rise to the loquacious young gentleman's
remarks at the opening of our story.

But Alice's thoughts were far back in the past.
She had been visiting, on that dull November morning, the "green spots of her memory."   She had
stood once more by the little brown cottage, beneath
the shadow of the maples, and heard her mother's
voice, and felt her hand upon her head in blessing,
as of old.   But her cousin's voice had broken the
spell; and his last question, "Pray, what do you
read it for?" was still sounding in her ears.   Her
cousin's sudden entrance, and her own sad thoughts,
made her nervously sensitive; and, when she
looked up, her lip trembled, and her eyes filled
with tears.

"Now don't, cousin, for the world, go to crying,
for I do hate scenes;" and Fred strutted conse-
quentially around the room.   "But, Alice, what is

the matter ? Are you really unhappy ? " said he, in an altered tone ; for, as we have already said, he had an affectionate disposition.

"No, no, Fred! not that: but I feel sad this morning; for I have been thinking about my own dear old home, and my father and mother, and the red school-house, where I used to go ; and, oh! so much-that used to be, and never can be again."

"Well, well, coz! don't fret about it! It's only the weather that makes you feel so. Come, cheer up! You're a little too blue at times, to be sure ; but, for all that, I like you first rate, — a deal better than I do Ada and Liz."

Alice fixed her large dark eyes upon her cousin beseechingly, — "Don't, Fred, talk so about your own sisters. I am sure they would not be cross if you did not tease and worry them."

"I don't care! they deserve it all! Don't you suppose I've seen how selfish they are? I say it's a mean shame ; and, while I'm at home, I'm going to take your part, and be your knight-errant. That, you know, is what they used to call the man who protected the ladies in old times," said Fred, patronizingly.

"Thank you, my dear cousin. You have always been kind to me, and I love you for it; but don't let's talk about this any more. I want to ask your advice about something, — an important project of mine."

Once more Fred's eyes were wide open with wonder; but he said nothing, and Alice proceeded, —

"I should have asked your mother about it; but you know Aunt Emily seldom. talks much to me, and somehow there don't seem to be any one who will listen to me as you do.

"You know when Uncle took me away from my old home, five years ago, I knew very little, — only the rudiments of reading, writing, arithmetic, and a little grammar."

Fred wondered what was to come.

"Since that time I have never been to school. But you, who have had all the advantages of education, cannot tell how I have longed for books and knowledge. Encouraged by Uncle William's kindness, I was bold enough to ask him to let me come here and read. He consented; and from that hour it has been my chief delight to occupy my leisure moments in this manner, and to make up by diligent study for what I have lost."

"Well done, Alice!" interrupted Fred. "I should call that 'the pursuit of knowledge under difficulties.' I think you're a model of thought and industry. Here I've been at school two years, and 'twould puzzle a lawyer to find out what I've been doing, except to spend money and waste my time; and all the time you've been wanting to learn so much! How I wish you had had the instruction that has been wasted on me!"

"Thank you, Fred; but you haven't heard my plan yet."

"Oh, no! I forgot. Pray proceed."

"But you won't laugh at what I'm going to say?"

"No: I'll give you my word beforehand."

"Well, the other day as I was looking over the books I took down one called 'Anecdotes of Self-made Men,' and I thought if the men it spoke of there could undergo so many hardships and sacrifices to acquire education, why could not I do something towards educating myself. And so I thought, and thought, and at last I hit upon a plan; but I'm almost afraid to tell you now, for fear you will laugh at it, or tell Aunt Emily, or do something else to spoil it all."

"No, I won't. You *must* tell me now, for I've got interested."

"Well, my plan is this: If Uncle William would advance money sufficient to pay my tuition until I am able to teach, I would then most cheerfully return it, — and then I would be fitted for usefulness. What do you think of it."

Alice's eyes brightened with hope as she spoke. Fred looked at her a moment, as if too much amazed to speak.

"Why, Alice Morton, are you crazy? What *did* put such an idea into your head? It's well you did not say any thing to mother about it. Why,

Alice, do you suppose father would allow you
to become a teacher or governess, subject to people's caprices or whims?   Besides," said he, as he
noticed her look of disappointment, "father is able
to send you to school a century if he is a mind
to.   I am going down to the office this very morning, and will ask him about it, if you wish."

"But then it would not be like earning it myself," said Alice, who could see no impropriety in
her discarded plan.

"I know it; but then it would be a much easier
way."

"But what real harm would there be, should I do
so?" persisted Alice.

"Why, not any that I know of, if your friends
were not able to do for you.   Father is not nig-
gardly, and will not suffer you to do such a thing.
But, suppose there was a necessity, and you should
do so, it would be a long time before you would be
able to pay for one year's tuition.   It will be years
before you can command a salary ; and the majority
of female teachers rarely get over three hundred
dollars a year."

Alice's countenance fell with the castles she had
been building in the air.   "But never mind," said
her sympathizing cousin, "I'll ask father about it.
He will arrange it right, I dare say."

So occupied had they been with their conversation, that they did not hear a quick step in the hall, or notice that the door which Fred had left ajar had been pushed slyly open, till a pair of angry blue eyes were fixed upon them, and a loud voice exclaimed, —

"I should like to know, Alice Morton, how you came in here. You have no business in father's private room. He'd be very much displeased if he knew it!"

"Uncle William gave me permission," timidly ventured Alice.

Here Fred interfered. "It wouldn't hurt you, I'm thinking, if you came here once in a while, instead of wasting your time in bed. Besides Alice *did* have permission. I heard father when he gave it to her ; and I say she shall stay if she wants to."

"You don't know any thing about it, and it's none of your business!" retorted his sister.

"My dear sister," said Fred, with mock gravity, "you remind me of the dog in the manger, who would neither eat the hay himself nor allow anybody else to."

With a frowning brow and an angry toss of the head, Lizzie retreated towards the hall, and passed on to the breakfast-room.

As the door closed violently behind her, Alice said, "Oh, Fred! how could you? It only makes things worse! I would much rather have gone out. But did you really hear uncle say I might come

1*

here? He told me the other day, and I thought we were all alone."

"No, I didn't hear him! I only told her so."

"But that was telling a lie."

"Oh, no! it was the most harmless thing in the world. Only the smallest kind of a white lie. I did it on purpose to spite her. You know lying is necessary in some cases."

"No! I don't think so. We never should do wrong, whatever good may come of it."

"But Liz is so obstinate and provoking; and then nobody expects me to be as good as you are. However, I'm sorry I told a fib. Good-bye. I'm going down to the office now."

"But you aren't going to ask Uncle William about that?" said Alice.

"Yes, I am. And you'll go to school, and get to be very wise or wonderful, and we shall all be proud of you."

So saying, Fred bounded out of the room, and Alice, with a sigh, put up her book, and went into the breakfast-room, to endeavor to pacify the still angry Lizzie.

CHAPTER II

ALICE MORTON was an orphan. For five years she had not known a mother's care or affection, and eight years had elapsed since she had climbed her father's knee, or received his coveted kiss. . Stern poverty and severe misfortunes had rendered her an inmate of her uncle's family; but she had never been happy there, and she had now only the memory of a home. But very pleasant was the memory of that home far back in the past. In one of the most beautiful spots in the valley of the Connecticut, far removed from the great city of trade, where the sun shines alike upon the dwellings of rich and poor, and where the flowers have leave to grow, was the peaceful cottage of Edward Morton, the carpenter. An honest but hard-working man was Edward Morton; and, as he went day by day to his simple labor, he never dreamed of being ashamed that he was a mechanic, but in the riches of his great heart thanked God for the blessings of health, freedom, and abundance.

- But trials came to that humble roof. Work became scarce, wages were low, and bread dear; and for the first time poverty crossed the threshold of

that quiet home.   It was at this time that the discovery of gold in California made it the Eldorado
of the traveller and adventurer.   The almost fabu-
lous stories told concerning the beauty of its climate,
and the richness of its veins of gold, appealed strongly
to the imagination of Mr. Morton ; and he departed
for that distant clime, strong in the hope of the uncertain future, and followed by the prayers and
blessings of his wife and child.

But poverty is a hard task-master, and Mrs. Morton was constitutionally delicate.   For two years
there came to them letters filled with encouragement
and counsel, and with words breathing hopes "of
better days."   Then came a long silence, and at
last vague reports of his death in a foreign land,
till at length her health sank beneath the added burden of labor and anxiety.

And was there no brother or sister or friend to
whom she could appeal in this her hour of extremi-
ty?   Yes, she had one sister ; but time, circum-
stance, and their own dispositions had rendered them
almost strangers.   As the wealthy Mrs. Whiting,
how could she be expected to visit the low, vulgar
mechanic's wife, even if she were her own sister?
So reason the rich.   While Mrs. Morton, with that
high-souled independence which belongs to a sensitive nature, shrank from asking aid of her unnatural
relative.

Yet, as she felt herself descending into the "valley of the shadow," when she saw the troubled waters of Jordan at her very feet, and thought of her helpless orphan Alice, she was constrained to make one last appeal. '

Very great was Mrs. Whiting's consternation upon the receipt of her sister's letter. If she refused her child a home, society would condemn her; and Mrs. Whiting was a fashionable, heartless woman of the world, and an utter slave to its opinion. But her husband's more feeling heart had been touched. Away down in the depths of that proud man's heart, there were some healthful springs which the hot breath of worldliness had not yet dried up; the rock had been touched, and the waters gushed forth. And he mentally resolved that he would bring the little orphan to his home, and love her as his own.

Alice never forgot the deep, earnest tones of her mother's voice, nor the soft pressure of her hand upon her head, as she pronounced her dying blessing upon her. And it may be pardoned Mr. Whiting if a few soul-felt tears stole down his cheeks, when, with all a mother's careful solicitude, she commended Alice to his love, and prayed him to keep her "pure and unspotted from the world."

But it is true that we are more or less influenced by our surroundings; and could that anxious mother have known the unhealthy moral atmosphere her child would breathe, and the hourly trials of temper

to which she must be subjected, she might well
have trembled. For, oh! how different was the
home of the millionaire, with its luxury, pride, and
discontent, from the little brown cottage of the carpenter, which once echoed to the cheerful song of
labor, and to the words of thanksgiving and praise.

So thought Alice, as she sat in her uncle's elegant parlor, on that rainy November evening, just
five years from the time of her mother's death.
The heavy curtains had been drawn before the bay-
windows, the anthracite glowed cheerfully in the
grate. It was that dusky time, between daylight
and evening, when one loves to dream by the dancing
firelight; and the members of Mr. Whiting's family
were enjoying it in their own peculiar way.

Alice, entirely hidden from view by the window-
curtains, had her face pressed close to the glass, and
was trying, by the uncertain light, to finish the page
she was reading, or anon glancing among the gath-
ering shadows for the coming of her uncle; for
Alice loved him with a sincere affection, and had
learned to watch eagerly for his returning footsteps.

She had an interesting face, although one at first
sight would not call her beautiful. Her brow was
high and open, with a look of frankness. Her eyes
were a clear hazel, and her hair a wavy chestnut
color, which clustered in short ringlets around her
neck. Her features were clearly defined, and a nose,

whose contour was decidedly Roman, gave a look of much character to her face. Added to this, her mouth was marked by lines, half of firmness, half of sweetness, and was constantly changing in its expression. Strangers always looked at her twice, as if something new attracted them each time.

Before the fire, in a luxurious rocking-chair, sat Mrs. Whiting, still a prey to the *ennui* of the morning. An expression of fretfulness was upon her face, which should have been lighted up with a smile of contentment, for of all earthly comforts there was not one she lacked. But —

"Who can minister to a mind diseased?"

With all her blessings, Mrs. Whiting believed herself the victim of all sorts of evils. "No one sympathized with her feelings." Her husband seldom sought her society. Her children were ungrateful, her servants untrustworthy; and she, as she declared herself, was "completely borne down by the burden of domestic cares."

The fact was, Mrs. Whiting was eminently selfish; and, in her complaining moods, she seldom thought that she made no efforts to please her husband; taught her children no principles of right and duty, which should lead them to respect and honor her; and seldom vouchsafed a kind word to her servants, to render them respectful and obedient.

Upon this day, in particular, every thing had combined to try her patience and temper. The rain had prevented a visit of a few of her " choice friends ; " her head ached unmercifully ; and she had been obliged to visit the kitchen *twice*, to hasten the dilatory servants, and to enforce her orders.

"Fred," said she, as the servant who had lit the gas retired, " has Ada returned yet ? "

"No, mamma ; and it's after seven. What can be the reason ? "

" It's just as I supposed," answered Mrs. Whiting ; " that rascally coachman didn't go for her. He said he should not. But I did not think he would dare disobey, after what I said to him."

" But, mother, what could be the reason John did not do as you bid him ? " asked Fred.

" Oh ! he had a nice long story about his father's being sick, and he must needs go and see him this very night. And, when I urged the necessity of Miss Ada's coming home to-night, he answered, that it was a case of life and death, — he must go."

"Of course you did not urge him after that, mother ! "

" Of course I should not, if it had been any trustworthy person," answered his mother, with a little secret complacency at seeing so readily into the character of her servants, " of course not ; but then one never knows when to believe these people. I dare say there was some frolic he wanted to attend.

And I told him he should certainly be discharged if he dared disobey my commands."

Fred wisely forebore to say any thing; but he mentally resolved that he would plead John's case with his father, if the worst should come to the worst.

"Well, at any rate," he answered, "John has not been; for I've just come from the stable, and the horses have not been out of their stalls this afternoon; so I will harness up the pony, and go in the chaise after Ada."

Alice heard the words of her aunt with fear and trembling, lest her threats should be carried into execution. Of a sweet and winning temper, and gifted with a large sympathy, she ever participated in the sorrows of those around her. On this afternoon she had gone to the kitchen to give John his customary lesson in reading, and to point out some precious passages from the Bible. She had heard the altercation between her aunt and him, and witnessed his anguish and despair when she refused his request.

"Oh, Miss Alice!" he groaned, "what shall I do? My father is just alive! I must see him once more, and I cannot lose my place."

"Poor John," said Alice,— all her sympathies speaking in her voice, — "I am so sorry for you! I will ask aunt to forgive you. Put your trust in

God. He has promised to make all things work together for good to them that love Him."

Many were the warnings given John by the servants in case he should disobey. But filial love triumphed over self-interest, and he went.

Alice had become very much interested for him. "How should I feel," thought she, "if my father were dying, and I could not perform for him the last offices of love?" But the task of Alice was harder than she had thought. She had invented all sorts of excuses for lingering in her aunt's room, fearing to approach the subject. Never at any time feeling free in her presence, now dreading her displeasure, —a wall of fear and coldness seemed suddenly to have risen up between them. Several times she attempted to speak, but failed of utterance. The evening found John's absence discovered, and her appeal unmade. "I will wait till Uncle William comes home," thought she, "and that will be better still."

CHAPTER III

THE THREE WISHES.

THE click of the night-lock was heard in the front door, and with a few of Mr. Whiting's brisk steps he had passed through the hall, and entered the drawing-room.

"Ugh!" he exclaimed, as he spread out his hands before the fire, "they do say, wife, that this is the most stormy November within the memory of the oldest citizen. But come, Lizzie," he added, "take your father's wet coat down to the kitchen, and let it dry."

"I'll ring for Netta, father?" said Lizzie inquiringly, moving towards the bell rope.

"No, no, child!" but, before Mr. Whiting could finish, Alice sprang eagerly forward, —

"O uncle! let me. I would be so pleased to go!"

As Alice's light footstep was heard departing on her errand, the careworn father turned towards his daughter with a sad smile, —

"I thought you would like to do me this small favor, my child."

"But, father," said Lizzie deprecatingly, "I was busy; and besides it is so unpleasant to perform such menial offices."

" It is never menial to minister to the happiness or comfort of those we love," said Mr. Whiting.

It was not the fault of Lizzie's heart so much as of her education, that she gave this unfeeling reply. Her father felt this, and once more resolved within himself that Alice and Ada should never receive a fashionable education. The idea that her father would have been pleased if she had shown him this slight attention never seemed to enter her head; but she turned again to her worsted-work, slowly bringing out the tomb of Napoleon, under a very green and very drooping willow.

But, besides Alice's natural kindliness of heart, another thing prompted her to visit the kitchen. She wanted to see her uncle alone, and thought this would be a favorable opportunity for escaping from the parlor.

Accordingly, when Mr. Whiting went down to tea, he found his niece in the dining-room ready to receive him.

" Well, little Miss Sobriety," said her uncle, " what brought you here ? " .

" I had something to tell you, Uncle William."

" So-ho! you did! and what may your august pleasure be ? Come, I will be your good fairy, and for the favor you did me will grant you any three wishes you may make."

" Will you ? Are you really in earnest, Uncle William ? " cried Alice in delight.

"Take care, Alice; no true fairy ever allows his word to be doubted," said Mr. Whiting with playful dignity. "Yes, I will grant you any request within the scope of my magic."

Alice's first request was different from what her uncle had expected. Fred had been as good as his word, and told his father of Alice's hopes and projects; and he had thought that her first request would be, that she might be sent to school. When, therefore, with half-childish eloquence, she told the story of poor John, and poured forth an appeal in his behalf, her uncle looked at her in surprise and admiration.

Alice's face was not one you would have called beautiful in repose; but when, as now, the soul shone through and irradiated it, it endowed her with that higher beauty, — the beauty of expression.

A tear stole down her cheek, and she looked at her uncle beseechingly, as she said, "You'll forgive John this time, wont you, dear uncle?"

"It wouldn't do, I suppose, to resist such skilful pleading. But why should you care about John? What worked your little heart up to such a pitch of sympathy?"

"Why you know, uncle, John is so clever, and so grateful if any one does any thing for him; and he's pious too, — he loves dearly to hear the Bible read. And do you know I'm teaching him to read, so that he can enjoy it all the time?"

Mr. Whiting's conscience smote him ; for he knew that in his family the Bible, of all books, was least read. But Alice continued, —

"And another thing, uncle : you know we should always be kind to the poor. And I couldn't help loving John, and feeling sorry for him, as he sat there so desolate, and his father dying not a stone's-throw from the house."

"But how do you know it was so ? Perhaps John made up that story to get off. How's that ? "

"No, no, Uncle William ! he told the truth. I am sure of it, for I could see it in his eyes."

"Well, well, Puss ! You'll learn the ways of the world soon enough. But what do you think aunt would say to this ? "

"Would she be very much displeased, do you think ? Oh, uncle ! I didn't tell John to go ; but I pitied him very much, and I told him I would ask Aunt Emily to forgive him. Was I very wrong ? I meant to do right."

Mr. Whiting could not answer. More melting than any pleading was this childish love and sympathy. Involuntarily he drew her closer, and realized more and more how dear she had grown to him.

"But come, my dear," he said ; "let's have the second wish. It's time you thought of yourself."

This time Mr. Whiting's expectations were fully met. Alice acknowledged her longing for knowledge ; her wish to go to school ; and her hope to become a teacher, that she might make herself independent of the world, and by the cultivation of her talents render herself of active use to those around her.

"You are right," he responded. "Nothing will be of so much value to you. Wealth weighs nothing in the balance. He who is morally and intellectually great is the peer of kings; and no man shall say to him, 'I am greater than thou.'"

"I know, my dear uncle," said Alice, "that you have done every thing for me,—fed and clothed me all these long five years; and I thought if I could be a teacher I might repay you a part of your kindness."

"Say no more, Alice; you shall go. I had already made arrangements to send you and Ada to school, and you will commence early next month. There, there!" he added, as Alice covered his face with kisses, "don't eat me up! All I ask of you is, that you will improve your time, and repay me by your industry and good conduct."

Alice took her uncle's hand; and, as they left the dining-room, he said to her,—

"But, my dear, you have forgotten your third wish. What shall it be?"

"Indeed, indeed, uncle," replied Alice hesitatingly, "I don't know,—unless it be that you and Aunt Emily and my cousins would love me more; and that our Heavenly Father may bless you for your goodness, and make me worthy of it."

There was an unusual moisture in Mr. Whiting's
eyes, and he patted Alice's shoulder approvingly.

" You are a good girl," he said, " and deserve to be
loved as you are.   If you don't think of any thing
you would like to-night, you can wait till to-morrow,
and tell me then.   Come, here we are at the door ; "
and he turned the knob, and entered the drawing-
room.

Mrs. Whiting half roused herself from her doze,
and asked her husband what had kept him so long.

Fred and Ada had returned.   The evening it
seems found Fred with his appetite for fun in no
way diminished.   He sat on a low stool behind
Lizzie's chair, slyly tying together the ends of her
balls of worsted, and watching for an opportunity to
fix a noose around her foot, knowing it would annoy
her in case she should rise.

Ada sat at the piano, idly thrumming away upon
the keys.   Her mind was wholly occupied with
thoughts of Lily Cushing's farewell party, which
was to be given on the eve of her departure for
school.   When Alice came in, she stopped playing,
and commenced talking to her.   Alice was obliged,
for the next half hour, to listen to an extended
account of all the arrangements, and answer Ada's
hundred and one questions.

" You can't imagine, Alice," said Ada, " what a
splendid affair it is going to be.   There are to be
tables set in Mrs. Cushing's long hall, with black

2

waiters to tend them ; and the invitations are to be written on the finest gilt-edged paper, with perfumed envelopes. The company are to be very select and *recherche*," — Ada had a smattering of bad French,—"and I've no doubt the dresses will be elegant. You ought to see Lily's. It's a beautiful rose-colored satin, with a white overdress, trimmed with the most expensive valenciennes lace. What shall I wear for a dress, Alice? I hope pa'll get me something splendid. What do you think of it, Cousin Alice? Don't you wish you were going? Perhaps I'll ask Lily to give you an invitation," said the condescending Ada.

"Really, Cousin Ada, I don't know which of your questions to answer. I think it is all very fine, and I should like to go very much ; but you know I am quite a novice in company, — I never attended a fashionable party in my life."

"But for all that," exclaimed Fred, "there would not be one there who could match our Alice ; for she possesses the secret of all true politeness."

"And, pray, what may that be ?" said Lizzie.

"The beauty of a refined mind, tempered by a loving-kindness to every one."

"Quite a poetical definition. What a pity Master Fred Whiting didn't practise that kind of politeness ! "

"I do, in spirit, sister ; but my love of fun prevents the fulfilment of the letter."

"A poor excuse is better than none, I've heard. For my part, I don't think natural qualities of mind and heart ever made up for a fashionable education and advantages."

"What are you thinking of, Alice?" said her uncle, playfully; for she had been looking into the fire very steadily for the last few minutes.

"It is just five years, to-night, since mother died,"' said Alice.

"My poor child! How thoughtless in me not to remember it!" Then, drawing his chair closer to his niece, he said in a low voice, —

"Do you remember, my dear, the night of your mother's death? With her last breath, she prayed me to keep you 'pure and unspotted from the world;' and invoked a blessing upon you.

"But I fear she placed her dependence upon a broken reed; for I was too much a man of the world, and could spare no time for the moral improvement of myself or family. You are old enough now, Alice, to understand these things. Your mother meant that you should be a useful Christian woman, who should make the world better for her having lived in it. I wish to see you fulfilling her desire. With industry, and a high courage, you can perform the allotted work."

"And with the help of God," said Alice, reverently.

"Of course, under the direction and blessing of

Providence." But Alice sighed; for she knew that her uncle, with all his riches, turned away from those " unspeakable riches " which are the best inheritance of the poor. Truly the Word says, " There is that maketh himself rich, yet hath nothing; there is that maketh himself poor, yet hath great riches."

It was a long time, that night, before Alice closed her eyes in sleep. A new future had opened before her, and she caught glimpses of a brighter day. And when, at last, sleep descended like a benediction upon her, it brought to her pillow only dreams tinged with the rose-hue of happiness and of hope.

CHAPTER IV.

LILY.

THE winter term, at Newton Seminary, commenced early in December; and it was now the middle of November. Mrs. Whiting had reluctantly consented that the girls should attend a plain New England school, though she had strongly urged that Ada should attend a French Boarding School. But her husband was firm. There was much hurry and bustle all over the house, for the wardrobe of the girls was to be prepared for a long absence from home. Ada had been reconciled to the idea of a country school, as she called it, by learning that Lily Cushing was to attend the same one ; and Alice was as happy as possible in the fulfilment of her dreams. She had already imagined the appearance of the seminary, built a thousand air-castles, and resolved on many a plan for her future course. The time also drew near for Fred to return to his school. It would be his last term before entering college.

Black John, the coachman, still remained with the family ; for, to do Mrs. Whiting justice, she had not thought his father was sick, when she threatened him with dismissal.

One day, as Alice was preparing for dinner, she

heard Ada at the head of the stairs, calling to
her, —

"Only look, Alice," said Ada; "did you ever ·
see any thing half so beautiful as this silk? Mother
bought it for us to wear to Lily Cushing's party.
You and I are to have every thing alike; for I
heard father tell mother he wanted there should be
no difference between us. · You know I went with
mother this morning; and, on the way home, we
drove round by Mrs. Cushing's, and Lily's party is
to be given next week. The invitations for you
and I came this morning."

Thus Ada chattered on, unconscious that her
words had sunk below the surface of her cousin's
heart. But Alice stood in what Fred would have
called a "dark-brown study," thinking of all the
blessings that were heaped upon her, and wondering
if any man ever lived who was so good as her own
Uncle William. But she had been taught by a
pious mother that every good and perfect gift
cometh from above; and she knew that it was His
fatherly hand which smoothed the pathway of the
fatherless, and tempered the wind to the shorn lamb.

But it is time that we should say something of
Ada's friend, Lily Cushing. She was the daughter
of a lawyer, eminent for his talents and business
abilities. In wealth they were the equals of Mr.
Whiting's family, but in tastes, habits, and principles very opposite. ˉ Mr. Cushing was a man of

large and liberal views, of an active benevolence, and of sound principles, whose fountain-head was found in the Word of God. He believed that his wealth was given him that he might enlarge his sphere of benevolence; and, as a faithful steward, he dispensed of his bounty to the poor, hoping for nothing again.

Alice had been with Ada many times when she had visited her friend. She loved the quiet home-feeling which pervaded the house,—the warmth which was never found in the spacious halls of her own home. There was no rigid ceremony, no freezing politeness, but perfect good-breeding and refinement. She loved Lily's gentle mother too, for she made her think of her own.

Lily was fourteen years old, and was a most sensitive and shrinking child. Her disposition was sweet, and her temper mild. Alice and Ada thought they had never seen any one so lovely. She was the idol of her parents; and Mrs. Cushing had often said she feared her love for her was too passionate, and that she might be weaned from it by the removal of its object. Not only was Lily beautiful in mind, but she united with this those personal graces which win the praise of the world, and attract the eye of admiration. But Lily was one of those beings who are in the world, and yet not of it. She was full of that charity which "thinketh no evil;" and it seemed as if flattery came to her not so much to degrade as to make her white soul seem whiter still, in contrast to its own deformity.

As we have said, she was very prepossessing in appearance. Her complexion was very fair; her hair of that color so aptly described as "brown in the shadow, and golden in the sun." Her eyes were blue, and her whole face radiant with an expression of love and goodness.

There are some faces which we look upon to venerate; but Lily's was one to love. It is true, such spirits seldom visit our earth; but they show us how pure our natures may be. They come to us like ministering angels, to lift us up as by a heavenly vision; to wipe off with the sweep of their white garments the earth-dust of worldliness and care.

CHAPTER V.

ON the morning of the day on which Lily's party was to be given, Mr. Whiting called Alice into his library. "My dear child," said he, "I have been waiting for you to tell me your 'third wish.' You know you were to think of it, and tell me what you liked best. Have you come to any decision?"

"Why no, uncle! Don't you remember I made it at the time? I wished that you would all love me; and I am very sure my wish is coming to pass."

"We have always loved you, Alice; but such good conduct as yours deserves some visible reward;" and Mr. Whiting threw round her neck a fine chain, with a gold watch attached. "I want, Alice, that you should prize this gift, not only for its utility, but for the lesson of life it teaches. Remember, that, every time this hand marks the hour, another hand is going round upon the dial of your life-clock, marking your deeds, 'whether they be good, or whether they be evil.' Try, my child, to think of these things: it is my great regret that I have put them far from me."

Alice said nothing; but her arm stole round her

2*

uncle's neck, and there was the sound of tears in her voice when at last she thanked and kissed him, —" I will keep your gift, dear uncle ; and its ceaseless 'tick-tick' shall remind me of the never-ending debt of gratitude and love I owe you."

All this time a very different scene was being enacted in the drawing-room. Lizzie was giving Ada her instructions for the evening. "Be careful, Ada," said her sister, "that you do not laugh aloud, for it is excessively vulgar. And, when you shake hands, present only two fingers, and bow slightly. You are so little accustomed to society, that I am afraid you will be rude. At any rate, do just as you see fashionable people do, and you can't help being right. But, above all, don't cultivate the acquaintance of anybody who is not well dressed and genteel. You are handsome and entertaining, and need not go a begging for friends."

And thus did this thoughtless sister infuse a moral poison into that young heart. Ada was naturally proud and overbearing, and should have been encouraged to be kind and self-sacrificing to others.

"Am I handsome ? " thought Ada, as she looked in her glass, for the hundredth time that day. Her mirror told a flattering tale, as it reflected back the clear complexion, glossy hair, sparkling eyes, and rosy cheeks of the young inquirer. But vanity is never contented with this silent testimony ; it wants

to hear of its charms from the lips of others. " Nobody tells me I am good-looking," said she aloud.
" I am going down to ask mother what _she_ thinks ; "
and the embryo belle ran down-stairs into the
drawing-room. But no one was there, save Alice,
who was sitting by the fire, mending an article of
dress.

" Do you think I am pretty, Alice?" said Ada,
impetuously.

" Why yes, cousin, quite. Why do you ask?"

" Because Lizzie told me so; and I wanted to
know what you thought. I wonder why people
don't tell me so to my face."

" But that would be flattery; and flattery is
always suspicious. Your false friends will tell you
of your good looks, when they have an advantage to
gain. For my part, I love you best when you are
good-natured and generous, and don't care a snap
for your good looks."

" Well, there's precious little comfort in you,
Alice Morton," said Ada; and she ran to find her
mother.

But her mother's thoughts were preoccupied
with a fresh novel; and there was no time to
attend to the spiritual needs of her child. So to
her teasing her mother answered, " Yes, dear, very
handsome!" and sunk deeper than ever in her
reading. And thus the good seed remained un-
sown.

How different were Alice's thoughts, as she prepared for the party that night! She was thinking of her mother's counsels, when she had attended a party once before. "My dear child," said that wise mother, "I will give you one rule, which shall be a sure guide for your conduct, — the secret of true politeness is true kindness. If your heart is filled with love for your fellow-men, you cannot fail to inspire them with respect for you. And let your thoughts and actions be natural; act yourself. The imitator either falls short of his model, or ridiculously overacts his part." Alice loved to remember these sayings, and apply them to her present needs; indeed she ever strove to regulate her conduct as she thought her mother would have approved. Let us leave the girls to their preparations, and find our old friend Fred.

He had gone to the stables to order the carriage, and was now having an animated conversation with Sam, the stable-boy.

This Sam was about twelve years old, — a farm-bred Yankee, — and given to white-lying of the darkest shade. Fred called him, familiarly, "Sam Patch."

"Don't you think I am irresistible, Sam?" said Fred, as he stroked the place on his chin where his whiskers would be, if he had any.

"Don't understand your French; but, if that long word means slick, must say as how I do."

"Now look here, Sam Patch, I want to know where my pearl-handed whip is."

"Dunno' nothin' 'bout it," said Sam, looking very innocent. This whip was a present from a friend, and Fred valued it highly. It had suddenly disappeared; and, knowing Sam's thieving propensities, Fred was bound, as he expressed it, to have it out of him.

"You'd better own up. I'll knock you into the middle of next week, if I find out you've been fibbing about this. You know where that whip is."

"Hope to die if I do!" and Sam crossed his hands upon his breast, and looked up with mock solemnity in the direction of the stars.

Finding threatening would not avail, Fred changed his tactics. It suddenly occurred to him what an extra joke it would be to take Sam with him to the party that night. "How it would shock Miss Ada, and my proper little cousin," thought he. "Done! I'll promise Sam that he shall go, if he'll own up about that whip."

"I say, Sam, did you ever go to a party?"

"Used to go to apple-parings and sewing-bees, when I was to home, if that's what you mean. Don't have no such good times now. Don't see nothin' but work an' nasty hosses from mornin' till night."

"Well, I am going to an apple-paring to-night, and if you'll own up about that whip I'll let you go with me."

"Told you I didn't know nothin' 'bout it," said Sam doggedly. "And then I haint got nothin' to wear, if I did go."

"I'll lend you my black necktie and my patent-leather boots."

"Will you? Wish I'd stole that whip, so's I could tell where 'tis."

"And I'll give you my last-summer's jacket, with shiny buttons," added Fred.

What farm-boy, who had never worn any thing but coarse garments made up at home, could resist such a temptation? For once in his life, Sam was strongly inclined to tell the truth.

"I guess," said he, "Black John must have taken it; for t'other day, as I was sweepin' out old Billy's stall, I happened to look up at the caves, and I seed suthin' stickin' out that looked 'xactly like the butt end of that whip."

Sure enough, as they looked up, they could plainly see the handle of the lost whip.

"You see," said Sam, venturing to break the ominous silence, "I put it there, so's 'twould be sure an' be safe."

"I thought you said Black John stole it," said Fred dryly. "But come up to my room, and you shall go with me. You've fairly earned it by the whopping lies you've told."

Fred sent a message to his sister and cousin, that circumstances would prevent his being present at the party till about the middle of the evening, and accordingly the girls drove to Mrs. Cushing's alone. Little did they dream of the mortification their mischievous Fred had in store for them.

At the party Alice saw many of her future schoolmates. The Newton Seminary was deservedly popular. The scholars were at home, spending their vacation; and many among them were the friends of Lily. The large rooms were brilliantly illuminated; festoons of flowers hung gracefully upon the walls, and from the ceiling above; and music and dancing enlivened the festive hours. In the midst of all this Ada moved like one in her element. Her handsome face and lively conversation made her the centre of a group of eager listeners. Her foot was lightest in the dance, and her laugh the merriest of any. Alice was more quiet, but modest and self-possessed. They wore dresses of dark blue silk. Alice wore the watch her uncle had given her. Ada wore a white overdress trimmed with valenciennes lace.

If Ada had been kind and thoughtful, she would have left her gay companions sometimes to entertain her less brilliant cousin, or to introduce her to her friends. But no: she thought of nothing but her own pleasure; and, if Alice had waited for Ada's attentions, she might have been a wallflower the whole evening.

"Ada," said Lily Cushing, "why don't you go and speak to Alice? She looks real lonely."

"Oh, I can't now!" was the reply, as she turned laughingly to her companions; "by-and-by, perhaps, I will."

But Lily wanted to see every one happy around her, and she did not selfishly exclude others from her enjoyments. An arm stole softly around Alice's waist, and a sweet voice whispered in her ear, "Are you having a good time? Come into the library, and let me introduce you to our friends."

Alice bowed her thanks; and, finding her cousin did not intend to notice her, she put her hand in Lily's, and allowed herself to be conducted into the library.

"I wonder who that pale, sad-looking girl is that is talking to Emma Weston," said Fanny Green, as they left the group who were clustered about Ada.

"Oh! that is Alice Morton; and she is Ada Whiting's cousin," said her companion; "Lily got acquainted with her at Ada's house, and thinks there never was one like her. Let's go and dance."

"No," said Fanny, "I think I will get acquainted with this Alice Morton. You know it is only common courtesy to entertain strangers; and then, who knows! perhaps I may entertain an angel unawares."

"Well, goodby!" replied the other; "for my part, I would rather dance than entertain even angels."

"Pardon me for speaking without an introduction: my name is Fanny Green."

Alice started at the strange voice; but the smiling face and bright eyes that met her view disarmed all prejudice, and she extended her hand frankly, and said, "And mine is Alice Morton, — shall we be friends?" The two chatted pleasantly of school affairs, and said they hoped they should both be in the same class.

"Ada," said William Cady, "where's Fred. I' haven't seen him this evening." Before Ada could answer the question, the object of their inquiry appeared to answer for himself. He had put his joke into execution. Amid a wondering silence, he conducted the strange visitor into the room.

With a low bow to Lily, he said, — "Permit me to introduce my friend, Samuel Lockling, from Connecticut."

"How d'ye do?" said Sam; "hope you're well."

Lily was much embarrassed; but with her usual kindness she gave a hand to each, and said, "Any of your friends, Fred, are welcome."

You have heard of the jackdaw that got among peacocks? Very much the same felt our hero. The company stood for a few moments in silence, gazing upon him as they would upon some strange animal suddenly dropped down among, them. In fact, Sam looked like a picture from the Comic Almanac. The necktie was drawn out into a bow of mammoth extension; the jacket, for which Sam had paid the price of his honor, just revealed a yellow shirt-bosom, fastened with very gay studs; while he carried his arms akimbo to prevent rumpling his stiff cuffs, which were folded over his sleeves.

But, for all his homeliness and lack of polish, he was a sharp-witted boy; and he began to suspect that a joke had been played at his expense. It certainly did not look like the apple-parings he had been used to. The rich dresses and jewelled hands of the young ladies little resembled the calico frocks and buxom looks of the country belles.

"I say, Fred!" said he, in a loud whisper, "where's the apples? Let's begin to pare!"

"I should say, Mr. Lockling," said James Pierce, with forced gravity, "that you were laboring under a delusion."

"What's that?" said Sam.

"A delusion, my friend," said James, proceeding in his grandiloquent way, "is an erroneous impression, which prevents the full play of the reasoning faculties, and produces an abnormal condition of the mind."

Sam was as much in the dark as ever. "He means to say," said Harry West, "that you've been gulled, — cheated: this isn't an apple-paring, but a social party."

"Don't believe it!" said Sam. "Nobody never cheated me yet. Anybody that takes me for a fool isn't much mistaken."

"That's a fact!" said one; "only you've got the cart before the horse."

"How could you, Fred?" said William Cady, in a whisper. "You have carried your fun too far this time. Ada feels dreadfully; and your cousin, almost a stranger here: how could you?"

"Nonsense!" said Fred; "Sam won't hurt any one. He's as harmless as a kitten. You may go and comfort Miss Ada, if you want to."

It must be confessed that this awkward scene had robbed Ada of her self-complacency. Her color came and went as she was repeatedly asked, "Who is he?"

"I declare," said she, "I don't know any thing about it. If Fred has a mind to introduce his friends here, he may own them; that's all I've got to say."

But Sam did not need attention; he was quite the "lion" of the evening. Every one had something to say to him. All seemed to enjoy the strange guest; and Sam, flattered by their attention, was as loquacious as could be desired. The company were too well bred to be rude to him; and his own mother-wit prevented his committing any serious blunder.

How quickly can the difference be seen between the true and the false lady! While Ada stood aloof, dreading lest Sam should recognize her, Alice, with true innate delicacy, strove to relieve his embarrassment. With the one wealth, position, and gentility could alone prevail; the other recognized a brother under any exterior, however plain, and obeyed the command, " Little children, lòve one another."

As it grew later, the guests began to depart; and Alice and Ada were both heartily glad when their carriage was announced. Acting upon Lizzie's suggestions, when Ada took leave of Lily she presented only two fingers, and bowed slightly, saying, " Good night, Lily."

Being wholly ignorant of drawing-room etiquette, our hero thought he could not do better than imitate her. So, awkwardly holding out his middle and fore finger he made a *fac-simile* of Ada's bow, and said, " Good-by, Miss! If ever you come up to Connecticut, jest inquire for Hezekiah Lockling's farm, and our folks 'll show you an apple-paring worth two of this. There's some difference betwixt hay and grass."

An *audible* smile ran through the rooms. Fred and his companions beat a hasty retreat to the dressing-room; and, once fairly on their way home, Ada burst into a fit of angry weeping, broken only by lamentations and bitter words of reproach. Fred whistled " Yankee Doodle;" Sam seemed concerned as to how he was coming out of the scrape; while Alice maintained a thoughtful silence.

At home Mr. and Mrs. Whiting were waiting the return of their children, as this was the last evening they would all spend together.

" Oh, dear! " sighed Mrs. Whiting, when Ada

had finished her list of Fred's enormities, "my
children will be the death of me! Oh my poor
nerves! And then just to think of the mortification
of the thing. William, that boy is going to rack
and ruin as fast as he can go. But you don't see it,
—none but a mother can; and my health so feeble.
But keep on, ungrateful boy! you'll kill your
mother, by-and-by, between you!"

"Emily," said her husband, "be calm. This is
the children's last night at home. Let it be a happy
one. I have learned that a little sunshine is better
than many frowns."

Mrs. Whiting sobbed convulsively, with her
embroidered handkerchief to her eyes. Ada cried
from sheer vexation.

"After so much thunder, there must needs be a
shower," said Fred; and the embryo Socrates went
to his chamber to relieve Sam not only of his
borrowed clothing, but of his anxiety.

Selfish, vain, indulgent mother! The soil that is
neglected produceth no fruit. "Do men gather
grapes of thorns, or figs of thistles?"

"Kiss me, mother," said Lily Cushing, as she
was retiring that night. "Only think, mother!
three whole months that I shall not hear your
'good-night,' or feel your kiss upon my cheek;"
and a few tears that would not be suppressed stole
down her face.

The soft glimmer of that night-lamp shed a me-

lancholy light over the chamber, and · revealcd a
touching scene. A kneeling mother prayed Heaven's blessing. upon her child, that wherever she
might go she might never stray from the Saviour's
fold.

" My child, in a corner of your small trunk you
will find a Bible, your mother's gift; read it daily,
and make it the lamp of your feet." And then, laying her hand among the sunny curls, she said
softly, —

" May the Lord love you, my Lily; may he lift
upon you the light of his countenance, and keep
you in his holy keeping now and for ever more ! "

Lily cried herself to sleep that night. Ada's
closely packed trunk stood in her room that night,
but if you had searched every corner you would
have found no Bible. There were ribbons and em-
broideries, gloves and perfumes ; but there was no
room for the Word of Life.

But from that unhappy home one prayer at least
ascended, and one altar smoked with the incense of
gratitude. To Alice's trusting soul the good Father
sent rest, and the Spirit of Love said "Peace."

CHAPTER VI

THE shadows deepened and deepened over the decks, and still Mr. Whiting and Alice sat in the twilight; she telling him of her love and gratitude, and he speaking words of counsel for the future. It was the New York boat bound out. The farewells had all been spoken, the city left far behind; but Alice sat looking tearfully at old John's last gift. It was a wooden pear tastefully carved, containing a purple satin heart, — the work of Content. That little gift told more of true sympathy and love than the costly jewels of kings; and it was more precious, — to one heart, at least.

Ada was in earnest conversation with a new acquaintance. Miss Evelina Cobb was a stylish young girl, who was returning to the Newton Seminary. She possessed the virtues of flattery and exaggeration in an eminent degree. Ada listened admiringly while she told her of her father's immense wealth, of the hundreds of balls she had been to, the beautiful dresses she wore. She had attended school at the seminary for some time, and Ada asked her how she liked it.

"Oh! I suppose all schools are alike," was the reply " They are all mean prisons. But, I tell you, they are awful strict at this school. And Miss Newton is a dried-up old maid; and she watches the girls as a cat would a mouse. I made a horrid fuss about going back; but pa said I was wild enough, and needed somebody to hold a pretty tight rein."

"Uncle," said Alice, "do you see that old man coming towards us? May I offer him my chair?" But, before Mr. Whiting could answer, Alice sprang eagerly forward. The old man had stumbled, and fallen upon the deck.

Evelina broke into a girlish titter.

"Are you much hurt, sir?" and Alice tenderly assisted him to rise, and placed his staff once more in his hands.

"No, little one: I thank you. There are few that would have done what you did."

"What a fool your cousin is to give that old man her chair!" said Evelina. "First come, first served, say I."

Ada did not like the heartless manner of her friend; but she had not the moral courage to denounce it. She thought her a stylish girl, and, strange to say, felt honored by her notice.

"Alice is a strange girl," she said. "I confess that I should not have done it."

Ada spoke truly. She would not even have thought of it. People who make self their idol are seldom over-thoughtful of the comfort of others.

" May I know my young friend's name ? " said
the old gentleman.

" It is Alice, — Alice Morton," was the reply.

" Morton ? — Morton ? " — he repeated, as if striving to brighten up some old memory. " Are you
any relation to the Mortons of Connecticut ? "

" My father once lived in that State. His name
was Edward Morton."

" Is it possible that this is Edward's child ? " said
the old man, looking earnestly in her face. " Yes,
yes. I see the same dark eyes and hair, the same
noble forehead."

" You knew my father, then ? " said Alice, in surprise."

" Bless you, child, yes ! He was my scholar for
years. And a promising pupil he was. Where is
he now ? "

Alice lifted her hand and replied, — " Gone to
that better country. I am a poor orphan, sir ; but
I am rich, too, for I have a father and mother in
heaven."

" My poor child," said her companion tenderly.
" Can it be ! I never heard of Edward's death."

" It is now eight years since he left us," said
Alice. " I can still remember how the tears stood
in his eyes when he bade us farewell. He rests in
foreign soil, — the golden sands of California."

" He was a good boy," said the old man thoughtfully, " and an honest man. I loved Edward."

8

"Then I shall love you," thought Alice, "for his sake."

Alice introduced him to her uncle, and told him of her future hopes. She was surprised to find that he was a resident of the same village where their school was situated. He had been to New York to obtain a permit for his grandson to enter the art-school. "I have a pet grand-daughter, too," he said, "and we hope to be able to send her to Miss Newton's school next term."

"What is her name?" said Alice.

"Ellen Lee."

"It is a pretty name," thought Alice. "I feel as if I should like her."

They chatted on until Mr. Whiting deemed it best that they should retire to their staterooms. The shadows of evening deepened over the boat; and, while it hides our friends from our sight, let us pay a hasty visit to Elmwood Village, and look upon another scene.

Beyond that sudden bend in the old road, on the other side of those great maple trees, stands the little brown cottage of the Widow Lee. Did you ever see a really old house, — one upon whose long gable roof the green moss had grown year after year? Such a one is this. The friendly grass grows around the low doorstep in summer; and the small window-panes, with their weather-beaten sashes, make it seem even more venerable.

The old-fashioned clock ticks in a corner of the large kitchen. It has swung its lazy round for half a century in that self-same place, and always looked upon a happy and loving family. It is an humble, yet neat apartment. The walls and floor are bare, save a few sketches on the walls, and a strip of faded rag carpet before the stove. An elderly lady and her daughter sit knitting by the light of a single candle; and once in a while the young girl will stop to pat the great house-dog curled up at her feet, or cast an affectionate look on her brother. Charles Lee and his sister Ellen are the widow's children, and her only treasures, save an honest name and a sure faith in God.

Charles flung from him the book he was reading, and, looking sadly at his mother, exclaimed, "Oh, dear! it is so hard to be poor, to feel this terrible griping poverty in the way of every aim!"

"So I have thought a great many times," said Ellen; "but I never said it before. It don't seem quite right to complain."

"My children," said their mother, "what we lack in worldly goods is usually made up by an increase of spiritual riches. The great world beyond is full of snares, and riches are a pitfall to the feet of him that hath them."

"But there's Evelina Cobb — that proud girl that ridiculed me so last summer — has as much money as she can spend. Now, why is she permitted to waste it when Charles and I need it so much ? "

" Do you mean that girl that laughed at your thick shoes, when you were driving old Brindle home last summer, and called you a ragged cow-girl, because you had a hole in your dress ? " said Charles.

" Yes : do you remember it ? "

" I shall never forget it. I don't think I ever felt so wicked in all my life. I felt as if I should like to kill her. And I was just going to call her a hard name, when something whispered in my ear, ' Charles Lee ! stop and think ; ' and then I remembered the morning's lesson, — ' not railing for railing, but contrariwise, blessing ; ' and so I said nothing, but let her go away. I tell you, Ellen, if I live I will paint that picture one day."

Charles Lee was no common boy. No one could look upon his frank, manly countenance, and not be struck by the high expression it wore. His mind was naturally brilliant ; but it had been softened and refined by home influence. He was spirited and daring ; but a mother's prayers and counsels had curbed the fiery passions and enlarged the generous nature of her boy. Miss Newton, the teacher of the seminary, was much interested both in him and his sister. In Charles she saw the dawnings of no common genius, and she freely taught him all she knew of the art of painting ; and now she offered

Ellen a free seat in her school, and promised her she would do all she could to fit her for a teacher.

They talked long of their future. Charles was desponding. He thought of his poor mother, and that she would be left alone if he should go to the art-school. But Ellen was hopeful and happy. Mrs. Lee was anxious for both her children, but most of all for Ellen. She remembered her scanty wardrobe, the thick shoes which Evelina Cobb had ridiculed ; and she answered Ellen's eager questions, —

"My dear child, you must make up your mind to bear some disappointments. But Miss Newton is your fast friend, and I hope my Ellen has strength of soul enough to bear any thing for the sake of education."

"Indeed I have, mother ; and then I don't believe the girls will laugh at me, if I try hard to please them."

"You'd make twice as pretty a picture as any of them," said Charles. "Sometime I shall paint you, and then it will be as an angel, with a white robe, and a halo round the head. And I shall love to paint the Madonna, with her sweet face ; but I shall not copy Raphael or Rembrandt. My Madonna will be you, mother, with your brown hair and blue eyes; and I know those who look at it will think it is the face of an angel."

Mrs. Lee wept. She was proud to be the mother of so noble a son.

"See, brother! you have made mother cry. It is because we are poor, and you cannot go to the art-school."

"If I live, she shall not have to weep much longer," said Charles.

CHAPTER VII.

THE little village of Elmwood was an oasis in our great desert world. There was no factory hum, as there is in most of our New England villages; but, instead of the noise of spindles, Nature sang songs of joy in the voice of the brooks, or grand triumphal hymns in the dim old pines which bordered the horizon like a verdant crown. It was a quiet, rural place, just fitted for a school, where no pleasures save Nature's tempted the students from their books. Miss Newton, the principal, was a lady of worth and talent, — a true Christian woman, and one of those rare persons who seem to mould and pattern the minds of the young after their own lofty and beautiful ideal.

Mr. Whiting communicated to her his wishes in regard to the girls' education. "I have brought them here," he said, "because your's is a plain New England school. I have sent one daughter to a French boarding-school, and she came back to me with all the healthful springs of truth and duty choked by vanity and self-love. I ask you to guard carefully the morals of these. Teach them obedience and generosity, if they learn less of Latin and mathematics."

Mr. Whiting spoke earnestly, as one would who had placed a priceless jewel in the keeper's hands. Miss Newton was much affected. " I will do what I can," she said; "but almost all depends on their early training. These girls have formed their characters in a great degree."

"Their home-life has not been what I wish it had," said Mr. Whiting. " I am a man of the world; and in the fashionable circles of New York the mind and heart are secondary things."

It was a large, cheery room into which our young friends were shown. The white beds nestled cosily under their snowy canopies; a pretty, though common carpet covered the floor; and pretty chamber chairs, bureaus, and sinks completed the furniture.

When Alice awoke the next-morning, the gray light was streaming in through the blinds. For a few moments she seemed like one in a dream, — hardly comprehending how she came in that strange room, and among those unfamiliar objects. Alice could not look back upon her former life with so much regret as did Lily, for she had had no kind mother to cheer and aid her; and the aunt who might have filled that mother's place had never tried to win her love. Alice's first emotions, therefore, were those of joy, that her ardent wishes were realized, and that her school-life was commenced. She reviewed all her past life. She remembered the little brown cottage which childhood's sunny memo-

ries still gilded with a sacred halo. Her feet went
over the same green paths. And she remembered
a sadder scene, — when she stood in a hushed room,
and wore a black dress, while strange hands lifted
her up to look for the last time on the pale face, ere
the " dust to dust " hid it for ever from her sight.
And then came a new life in the great city, — a
beautiful house, splendid furniture, rich dresses,
and gay company; but how gladly would she have
exchanged it all for a mother's love or a father's
blessing! Yet there are bright spots in every experience; and Alice felt that many gleams of sunshine
had checkered her city life. She thought with
pleasure of the good she had done " Old John,"
and called to mind her Uncle William's kindness,
and Fred's sympathy. " After all," said she to herself, " if it had not been for Fred, I never should
have come to school. He did not laugh at my foolish plan, but helped me to a better. Oh! I do love
him and Uncle William; and I hope I can do something to show it yet. Of course," she mused, " I
would not like that he should ever feel the need of
my help; but, if he ever should, I should be so
proud and happy to show them that the poor orphan
could repay their kindness."

School-life had opened pleasantly to our young
friends. They learned to love their kind teacher;
and Alice looked upon her almost as a mother.
Only one thing troubled her, and this was Evelina

3*

Cobb's unhappy influence over Ada. None can tell how much a flattering, silly girl may mislead one of Ada's unstable temperament.

One day, as Alice passed a group of girls on her way to the dining-room, she heard Jane Swift talking in a very-mysterious manner. This Jane Swift was a gossiping girl, the bosom friend of Evelina. She loved dearly to retail every thing she heard; and a piece of news suited her better than a Paris bonnet. The girls called her the "Newton newspaper." When it was first known that our friends were coming to the school, she had seized upon the report with her usual eagerness; and she astonished her schoolmates by telling them of the lovely orphan, Alice Morton, whose father was devoured by lions in California, and whose mother died of a broken heart. But we have forgotten our story. Alice heard her talking in a subdued undertone, —

" I was in the anteroom, and I overheard the whole of it. You know Evelina came down this morning very late; and Miss Newton told her last term, that, if she was not early in future, she would have to go without her breakfast."

" What did she say to her ? " said Ella Richmond.

" Oh! she gave her a regular blessing. And she talked to her about her dress. But that isn't the worst of it. You know Evelina always had the greatest dislike to Ellen Lee, and is not backward about expressing it. It seems that last night Ellen overheard us talking about her, and heard Evelina call her a ' charity scholar.' "

" And she ran right off and told Miss Newton, I suppose," said Emily Dean.

" No, not quite that. Miss Newton found her crying in the dressing-room, and made her tell her what was the matter. I'm afraid she will call me to an account. Do you remember any thing I said, girls ? "

" No ! Did I say any thing ? " exclaimed all in a breath.

Anxiously they listened while Jane proceeded : —

" Miss Newton was dreadfully displeased. She told Evelina that Ellen Lee was now a member of the school, and she should allow no one to insult or wound her ; and she threatened her with dismissal in case the offence was repeated."

The girls talked on ; but Alice had heard enough. She saw the evil influence which Evelina exerted on those around her, and she felt sad that Ada should be attracted by her empty show and glitter. And she mentally resolved that she would try and win her back to the society of true friends.

Ellen stayed at noon, and took dinner with the rest. Her face was pale and sad, and she seemed nervous when spoken to. Shrinking and sensitive as she was, the rudeness of her schoolmates had wounded her to the quick. Could those thoughtless girls have seen her the night before, when she reached her home and gave free vent to her grief, they would have spared that young heart such anguish. But they were laughing and happy; while she, the butt of their ridicule, knelt in the little kitchen, and, burying her face in the folds of her mother's dress, told, with tears and sobs, the story of her school troubles. They did not see the tears in the mother's eyes, nor witness the fiery anger of Charles, nor hear the trembling voice of Grandfather Lee, as he blessed and encouraged her. How should they know or care? Were not they rich, and she poor?

CHAPTER VIII.

SPRING had come, with its soft breezes and flute-like melodies ; and with its awaking buds came also a new life to Frederick Whiting. He had passed his last term at school, and entered college with the most flattering prospects. He was young, rich, and handsome ; added to this were his polished manners, and strong, healthy mind.. No wonder that these many qualities made him a general favorite, and that he was in danger of being spoiled by flattery and admiration. In fact, Fred was in danger of becoming as flippant and frivolous as the butterflies of fashion who surrounded him. His room was the resort of gay young men,—" prime fellows," —whose list of accomplishments was only equalled by that of their demerits.

But Fred never failed in a recitation. His lessons were always ready; though no one could tell how they were prepared. Was there some convivial meeting of choice friends ?—there was Fred. · Was there some plan on foot for pleasure or amusement ? — there was Fred. Open, sunny-hearted, and generous to a fault, he was a ringleader in every boyish freak. ·Only one influence restrained him, and that was the counsel of his friend, William Cady. And sometimes, too, when on the eve of some new frolic, he would think of Alice, and laugh to think how gravely she would look and talk, if she knew of his doings.

"I tell you, boys," said Frank Parsons, one of a group of intimates who gathered in Fred's room one night,—"I tell you, it will be capital sport. We've got it all arranged. Next Friday night, the 'boss' and his satellites are going to a levee, so it will be a fine chance for us to take a holiday. We've fixed it so. Henry Mason has engaged to furnish us with horses and wagons from his father's stables; and at nine o'clock we will start for Cherry Farm, where a supper will be in waiting for us. I guess we'll waste the midnight oil to better advantage than in digging out Latin."

"But how shall we get back?" said another; "and how shall we excuse our absence?"

"Oh!" replied the first speaker, "we'll manage that. Wit is the twin-brother of necessity. We may depend on you, Whiting?"

"Certainly," was the reply; and they shook hands over their bargain, and departed.

Fred's room had been fitted up expressly for him. A Brussels carpet covered the floor; rich, heavy curtains shaded the windows; and bookcases and busts gave a finishing touch to the beautiful apartment. When his visitors were gone, Fred took down his books, run over the lessons, and then sank into a fit of profound musing. He was in trouble. The projected frolic, to which he had pledged himself, would be a dangerous and expensive one. But the danger did not trouble him. It was only the latter consideration. His extravagant habits had left him destitute of funds. How were they to be raised? Scarcely a month had passed since he had received a liberal allowance from his father; and he knew if he applied again it would cause inquiries, and perhaps his allowance would be lessened in the future. It would not do to sell any article, for that would be sure to be discovered. But he could not refuse to go, his word once given; nor indeed could he forego the hope of so much pleasure. In this dilemma, a thought suddenly struck him. He rose hastily, went to his writing-desk, penned a letter, sealed and directed it. Let us look at the superscription. "Miss Alice Morton." Yes: he had applied to his cousin for money to help him out of this difficulty.

How eagerly did Fred break the seal of Alice's answering letter, which he received two days afterwards! He glanced at rather than read the following words:—

My Dear Cousin,—Your affectionate letter gave me a great deal of pleasure; but the request you made has caused me more pain than I ever experienced before. The money I can let you have without difficulty, as Uncle William's liberality overleaps my most extravagant wishes. Dear cousin, do not

think me presuming, when I ask you to think seriously before
you take this step. What were one little night of pleasure to
the disgrace, it may be of expulsion, or the pain of conscience?
I know you will respond when I appeal to your sense of right.
Think of the hopes that hang on your course! Think of your
parents' disappointment, if, instead of pointing to you with just
pride, they were obliged to view their only son in silent shame!
O my dear Cousin! think, reflect: the first wrong step of a
lifetime has often been a lesser one than this. You know me
too well to think I would object to a harmless frolic. But this
is not so. How mean to creep away under cover of darkness,
and in the absence of teachers! O Fred! how can you, so
noble-hearted, do any thing you would be ashamed the whole
world should know? You love me, do you not? At least I have
thought so. I love you; and I have prayed that I might speak
rightly in this case. I have sent you the money; but oh! Fred,
if you have any love for me, let me beg you will show it by
resisting this temptation. Will you not do this much to please
me? I shall wait eagerly for your answer. Meantime my constant prayers follow you. Ada sends love, and joins me in this
supplication.

Ever your loving cousin,   ALICE.

Fred turned the ten dollar bill over and over
again. The eager look with which he had received
it had vanished, and in its place was a look of pensive thought. Long he sat and mused. In his first
disappointment at his cousin's sober letter, he had
indulged in all sorts of bitter words, — called his
cousin old-maidish and stingy; but when he read
her earnest, loving letter over again, he was ashamed.
The letter and money dropped from his nerveless
grasp. The form of Alice seemed to rise up before

him : he could fancy her sweet, pleading expression, and almost see the tears in her eyes, and hear her voice, as she said, " Will you not do this much to please me ? " He thought how selfish he was to be willing to inflict so much pain on others for an evening's frolic."

" I would not go," he said softly, " if I had not given my word."

" But a bad promise is better broken than kept," said Conscience.

" No," replied the tempter. " Your honor is at stake. You have the money, — go."

But again the faithful sentinel, Conscience, whispered, " Be above it. Show you honor a manly sentiment, by refusing to stain it by deception."

Hard pressed, the tempter urged his strongest point, — " You will be called a coward. Your companions will ridicule you."

" I do love you, Alice," said Fred, " and I should like to please you ; but you ask too much. I cannot break my word."

" You have done right," said the tempter. " You have done wrong," said Conscience. " Count one step backward."

" I shall not go," said William Cady, in answer to the entreaties of his schoolmates. " I know my parents would object ; and my own heart tells me it is wrong."

" I have thought of withdrawing too," said Fred.

"What, you! Why, your name is on the list. What has come over you?" said one.

"Is it conscientious scruples, or does the old governor object?" said another.

"Oh! Whiting's turning Methodist," said Frank Parsons. "How long have you been on the anxious seat, Brother Whiting?"

The color of wounded pride rushed to Fred's temples. "You are too bad, boys," said he, laughing. "I did not say I *should* withdraw, but that I had thought of it."

Once more the tempter had triumphed.

Friday evening came. Fred had stifled down every feeling of self-reproach; and, if thoughts of Alice and her letter did intrude, he had put them out of his mind as soon as possible. The plan of the students was all matured. An empty house had been secured at Cherry Farm, a place about five miles from the city; an expensive supper was ordered to be ready when they arrived; and they only waited for darkness to cover their departure. There was a strong feeling of disapproval among the older students; and by no means the best class of them were engaged in the enterprise. The rules of the institution forbade the absence of pupils at night, unless by especial permission.

Fred retired to his room to prepare. Strange to say, the pleasure which he anticipated so joyfully a week ago now had no charm for him. He heartily wished the frolic was all over; for Conscience had never once ceased talking to him of right and duty. The party were to start at nine. Eight o'clock came, — half-past, — a quarter to nine; and still Fred sat in his room silent and unhappy. Alice's letter was on a table before him. Shall I tell you what was in his mind all this time?

As he sat there, half conscious, half dreaming, he was recalling much of his past boyhood. The little college room faded away before his eyes; and in its place he saw a beautiful room, with rich furniture and costly pictures. A merry, laughing boy, and his bright-eyed sister, played draughts in a corner; and an invalid lady sat in the sunlight, which poured its afternoon glory into the apartment. It was one of the pictures of his memory. But the foremost figure was a child, with eyes tearful and beseeching, and a face wearing all the expression of sorrowing love. How well did Fred remember that scene! It was when Alice first came to live at her uncle's. She felt lonely and desolate in the great room, and would often sit down and cry for hours together. Fred was at home but little, but he always liked the sprightly Ada better than the sober Alice. On this afternoon Alice had crept to the back of his chair to watch the game. She had been weeping, and the tears were not yet dry upon her cheeks. "Go away," said he rudely; "I hate cry-babies." All this came back to him as he sat there; and he could see her reproachful look when she said, "O Cousin Fred! I have no one to love me!" And then he remembered how with eager regret he had kissed her, and said he was sorry, and from that time loved her better than all the world. "I wonder," he thought, "if Alice would recognize in this selfish being the same frank and ardent boy of long ago."

And then another picture rose up before him. He fancied Alice in her room at school. He could see her kneeling, and praying that he, her cousin, might be "delivered from temptation." And then came the sweet pleading voice, — "Will you not do this much to please me?" His pride and self-love appeared to him in all their hateful deformity; and he said, "It is enough! Alice, your letter has saved me."

"Come, Whiting! what are you dreaming about? We've been waiting this ten minutes for you!" exclaimed Frank Parsons, as he slapped our hero familiarly on the shoulder.

"I am not going," said Fred firmly. "Not going! — not going!" was echoed from all sides. But, in spite of remonstrances or taunts, he held his purpose. The rubicon was passed, — he had reached the shores of peace and quietness; and his companions, with their dangerous project, were left on the other side.

Morning brought back the students, merry with wine. Fred looked at them, and rejoiced that he had escaped such degradation. The freak was discovered ; a part of the students were suspended, and the ringleaders expelled. Fred felt that he could afford to have Frank Parsons call him a coward.

And Alice ! was not she doubly happy when she read the affectionate letter her cousin sent her in return ? The influence she gained over him at this time was strengthened by future correspondence. Alice's conscientiousness was a check on his impulsiveness. Truly " there is that maketh himself poor, yet hath great riches." Poor, indeed, was she in this world's goods ; but rich in faith, rich in love, rich in moral influence over those she loved. Who would not rather prefer to be a blessing to others, — a monitor of good, — than to possess the world ?

The seed sown in prayer and in tears here bore its first harvest. It was the first sheaf in Alice's harvest of love.

CHAPTER IX.

SPRING budded, bloomed, and faded; Summer grew old in the steps of her elder sister, till, smothered by her own roses, she dropped them, brown and sere, into the lap of pensive Autumn. And yet another winter and spring have departed since our friends entered upon the pleasures and trials of school-life. Circumstances had rendered Alice mature, while yet a child; but now the discipline of hard study had deepened the thoughtful expression upon her face, and made her, in very truth, a woman. Gentle, loving Lily had worked her way into every heart; for her soul was like a wind-harp, vibrating to every passing emotion, whether of sympathetic smiles or tears. Beautiful she was as a spirit, and as pure; but as fragile as a flower. Whenever the girls had an angel to paint in their pictures they would give it the face of Lily; and they said their only fear was that she would steal its wings and fly away. But, for all this, her goodness was of the negative kind, passive and yielding. With Alice it was an active Christian principle; and she found the spur of duty in Christian love.

Long ago Miss Newton had separated Ada and

Evelina, for she saw the evil of their companionship. Ada had been advanced to a higher class. Between Alice and the thoughtful Ellen Lee a tender intimacy had sprung up; and much good to both was the result.

It was a sabbath morning in August. The dew yet lay upon the grass, and the sweet perfume of clover blossoms came in at the open windows like the sensible blessing of Mother Nature. A sabbath in the country! — how blessed is it! The great trees stretch above you their tall arms in benediction; and the ring of silver bells seems to speak of that heaven where all is one eternal harmony.

. It was a pleasant walk to the church. Alice found her little class assembled in the chapel. Many of them were the younger scholars of the seminary, and were tenderly attached to their Sunday teacher.

Evelina sat in her room. Her hair was yet in papers, and her morning dress unchanged. On her return home at the last vacation, she had supplied herself with a quantity of yellow-covered novels; and she now sat crying over a story of love and broken hearts. Jane Swift, now her room-mate, was standing before the glass, practising airs and graces. Evelina stopped reading to look at her, as, perfectly unconscious, she went through her performances. It was ludicrous enough. First she would smile in the most killing way, just enough to show the tips of her teeth; then she would draw down the corners of her mouth with becoming gravity; then, opening her fan, she waved it languidly to and fro, only stopping now and then for another of those melting smiles.

"What *are* you doing, Jane?" exclaimed Evelina.

"Nothing," said Jane, blushing, — "only amusing myself. What are *you* doing?"

"Oh! I'm reading the 'Robbers' Cave, or the Knight's Revenge;' and I've just come to a splendid passage where the lady is killed by the robbers, and the knight swears vengeance. Don't you think, Jane, that we live in a dreadful hum-drum age of the world? No one ever gets carried away by robbers now-a-days; and there are no knights to rescue fair ladies."

"And no one to play the guitar under the greenwood tree," added Jane. "But come, Evelina; get up, or you will be late to meeting."

"Oh! I don't believe I shall go," said Evelina, yawning. "Miss Newton won't notice that I'm not there among all the rest."

"But you know," said Jane, "that Judge Hall's son came home from Germany this week. So I suppose he will be at church this morning."

"Sure enough!" said Evelina. "I guess I will go."

"Miss Alice," said little Lizzie Grant, when the lesson was all repeated, "will you be so kind as to tell me what a 'catch' is?"

"I don't understand you, my dear. Tell me in what connection you heard it, and then, perhaps, I can explain it."

"Why, the other day Nelly heard Evelina talking about a Mr. Hall that had just come home from Europe, and she said he was a 'great catch.' Now I always thought a catch meant some kind of a trap, and we didn't see how a man could be a trap."

Alice blushed at the childish version of her schoolmate's remark, and briefly told them that it was a foolish saying.

"But the Bible says, Miss Alice," broke in the child, whose thoughtful blue eyes were fixed wonderingly upon her, "that it is the lips of fools that poureth out foolishness."

Alice could not say a word. What defence could she give Evelina? Even the pure lips of a little child had condemned her.

Down the aisle walked Alice to her accustomed seat. The village church was no costly structure; but a simple temple, cheerful and sunshiny, like the religion that was preached there Sunday after Sunday. The warm wind stole in through the open windows, eloquent with the smell of new-mown hay and golden fruits; the sunshine fell in broad bands across the nave; and the sound of brooks and whispering leaves thrilled the air like rippling music.

Alice's mind was filled with devout thoughts. As the organ pealed out its solemn tones, she

4

thought that the little church, with its nave resting
in sunshine and shadow, and its organ harmony in
the choir, was a symbol of what our life should be.
On the level of every-day life, duty and pleasure,
sorrow and joy, blend like the shadow and sunshine;

but, like the organ above, the soul's voices should be ever singing, to hallow the daily life alike of joy. or sorrow.

The minister preached upon "Vanity;" but Evelina did not hear a word.

CHAPTER X

"I wonder what it can be!" said Lucy Howard, as the old stage stopped at the door, and a large square package was handed out.

"I'll bet a copper I can tell!" said the ever-ready Jane Swift. "It's those Intellectual Philosophies that Miss Newton has ordered to bother our brains with."

"No," said Mary Knowles, "the package is too large for that."

Miss Newton ordered the mysterious article to be brought in and placed upon the table. "What is it?" exclaimed many voices.

"I don't know," she replied. "We will open it and see."

The girls stood in anxious expectation while the wrappers were removed.

"Oh, it is a picture!" said Lily Cushing; "I can see the corner of the frame."

"Yes," said Ada, "I can see it; it is an oil painting."

"How beautiful!" exclaimed all, as the last wrapper was removed. "Why, it is the old road. There are the old maples, and there is the bend, with the Widow Lee's cottage beyond; and even old Brindle," said one. " How perfect ! "

A note had dropped from the picture. It was dated at New York, and signed " Charles Lee." It begged Miss Newton's acceptance of the work, as a token of gratitude, and a sample of his improvement during the year and a half he had attended the art school.

Ellen gazed with admiration, not unmingled with pride, on her brother's beautiful work. He had written her that he intended sending Miss Newton a picture; but she knew not of the deep meaning he had hidden in it, — of the wounded pride which found expression in its lights and shadows, and of the spirit of revenge which had nerved the arm and guided the brush of the young painter.

" I do believe, Ellen," said Lily, " that he meant the milkmaid should represent you. And that boy coming over the field with the hoe over his shoulder looks just as Charles used to ! Isn't it beautiful, Miss Newton ? "

" It is indeed," replied their teacher. " I see no reason why Charles should not become a great painter."

As these things were pointed out to Ellen, a new light was cast upon the picture. She saw through the whole now. Charles had painted the scene beneath the old maples to revenge himself upon Evelina for the insult she had offered his sister, when

she taunted her with her mean attire and her poverty. She dreaded to have the girls discover the
truth, and yet she wondered that they could be so
blind.

"Why, girls!" exclaimed Lucy Howard, "those
faces are all portraits. Look at that figure — pointing towards it — it is the very image of Evelina
Cobb."

"Hush! there she is now," said Lucy, as Evelina entered the room and advanced towards the
group. "Don't say any thing. See if she will
notice the resemblance!"

"Look, Evelina! see what a beautiful picture
Charles Lee has sent us."

Evelina advanced towards the speakers. "I think
it is done very well," said she. But, as she took a
nearer and closer view, she saw something in it besides an old road with maples. Every line was alive
with meaning. It was no fancy sketch. That summer scene came back to her : the picture represented
her as she stood there, with her countenance scorn-
ful, her hand extended, and her lips just parted to
speak those cruel words, "You are a ragged cow-
girl." Covered with mortification and anger, she
looked round upon the group to see if they remembered the scene. She met the inquiring looks of
Miss Newton, and the conscious faces of her schoolmates. The color rushed to her cheeks, and then
retreated, leaving her very pale. Miss Newton,

surprised and alarmed, said, "You seem faint;" and made a motion to help her.

"No!" said Evelina, endeavoring to recover herself: "it is nothing." Her pride came to her aid.

"I don't care,—I am not ashamed," she said over to herself, as if answering the rebukes of conscience. "I always *did* hate Charles Lee. I hate him now. I hate his sister. Why should I fear to look at that picture? I *will* look at it!" and she fixed her eyes firmly upon the painting.

But the beseeching expression which Charles had thrown into those eyes,—the pleading humility,—were too much for her. She looked up, but only to meet those of the original fixed mournfully upon her face. It was a look of pain, as if she asked pardon for her brother's revengeful act. Pleading illness, Evelina escaped from the room.

"What is it?—what was the matter with Evelina?" asked a dozen voices in a breath. And twenty voices essayed to answer the question. Miss Newton was wholly ignorant of the case; and our friends looked on with eager curiosity. Ellen felt that she alone could put the act in its proper light; and she was anxious to tell the story herself. So, leaving the girls, she requested a private interview with Miss Newton.

"Isn't it romantic?" said the girls. "Who would have thought it? It's as strange as any thing we read in books!"

"Oh! but," said Jane Swift, "I think it was cruel in him to paint our portraits there! Only think of it! there they will remain for years."

"But only think," said Jerry Williams, "how much worse it is to wound two such sensitive hearts as theirs! This picture is engraved on their souls, and the memory of that cruel taunt will remain there for ever!"

"It wouldn't have been so bad," said Lucy Howard, "if one of you had been handsome. Then some one might have seen the picture and fallen in love with you; and that would have finished it up beautifully."

"You ought to have been there, Lucy," said Emily Dean.

The study bell rang, and the girls left the drawing-room. Two seats were vacant, Evelina's and Ellen's. A hush seemed to have settled upon the school, and the girls were dreamy and absent-minded.

Jane Swift managed, privately, to tell Ada that she was glad of it, and hoped it would cure Evelina's pride.

Alas! what pride so great as that which shuts its eyes to its own faults?

Between tears and sobs, Ellen finished her story. "My dear Miss Newton, I cannot tell you how sorry I am for this occurrence! It does not seem possible that my dear, good, generous brother would stoop to revenge an injury. But oh, madam! his provocation was great. He is high-spirited, and loves his unworthy sister as well as when we knelt together at our mother's knee. Let me pray that you will not let this rob him of your respect; for, oh! indeed he is good and worthy."

"My dear girl,"— and Miss Newton laid her hand soothingly on Ellen's heated brow,—"I am sorry and grieved, but not so much for Charles's act as for the heartless unkindness of the girls under my care. Do not distress yourself. Charles does not suffer in my regard; and I the more admire your sisterly love. But, when I think that these girls whom I have led and counselled, whose hearts I have tried to fill with the harmony of love, have gone astray into folly and selfishness, my spirit is troubled. I fear I never shall — never — be able to win them to the Good and True."

"Oh, indeed!" exclaimed Ellen, forgetting her reserve,— forgetting every thing in her eager love, —"I think you will ; I am sure you can. Evelina is giddy and vain, but I cannot think her heartless. Alice Morton says she has a soul somewhere, only it cannot breathe in the air of fashion and empty pleasure. Dear Alice! she is so good herself. She looks sad when Evelina talks to Ada, and flatters her."

"Alice Morton and Evelina Cobb are two opposites," said Miss Newton.

"But I think," said Ellen, suddenly recollecting herself, "that she will grow better by-and-by.

4*

After all," she said, with touching sadness, "why should I expect to be loved? I am poor and plain-looking, and reserved: no doubt Evelina thought I was proud."

"Ellen," said Miss Newton, "you know I never flatter my pupils; but I see you have been making yourself unhappy. Perhaps you need encouragement; so I will tell you something that I hope will convince you that the world respects merit and virtue as well as wealth and beauty."

Ellen looked gratefully upon her teacher, as she listened.

"You know, my dear child, your great object has been to fit yourself for a teacher. One-half of your school course is finished, and I have interested myself to ascertain if any school was in want of a teacher. I was not very successful here; but perhaps you remember a tall, dark-looking gentleman, who visited the seminary last week. He is the Principal of the Graham Institute, and he casually remarked that one of his female assistants would be married as soon as her engagement with the school expired. I showed him your written examinations, and was happy to give him a testimonial of your good character. He seemed perfectly satisfied, and said he had no doubt you could have the situation if you wished. So I engaged it for you, providing you consented. Come, Ellen, what do you think of it?"

She lifted her eyes, full of happiness and gratitude, and, springing from her chair, grasped Miss Newton's hand in silence.

"What have I done to deserve all this?" she said at last.

"All that you could do," was the reply. "You have been faithful and obedient, and I am pleased with you. There," she said, as Ellen gave vent to her gratitude and joy, "you may go to the school-room now; I wish to see Evelina."

"One word more, if you please, Miss Newton, — you are not displeased with Charles?"

"No, Ellen. It is true, I cannot approve the course he has taken; but I regard it as the expression of a high-spirited sensibility, which, if rightly curbed, would be a virtue."

"I fear, even now, you do not regard him as you did before," said the loving sister. "I don't think he ever would have painted that picture if Evelina had not ridiculed me the first day of the term. You should have seen him that night. His eyes flashed, his hands were clenched, and he paced the floor like a caged lion. I was frightened out of my grief by his anger; and it required all grandfather's persuasions to keep him from coming to see you directly."

Miss Newton saw that Ellen was distressing herself with these unpleasant memories; and with a smile of authority she pointed towards the school-room, while she herself sought Evelina in her chamber.

The door was unlocked; and, receiving no answer to repeated knocks, she entered. At first she
saw no one in the disorderly room; but presently
there was a movement at one of the bay windows,
and a curtain was pulled slyly aside. Evelina rose
when she saw who it was, and placed a chair. Her
eyes were red and swollen with weeping. Miss
Newton augured well from this, and hoped that
she had been led to see her selfish pride, and repent
of it. But when she began to question her, and
received for her kind words only now and then
a sulky monosyllable, she knew that she mourned
only for mortification and loss of popularity. Long
the patient teacher sat, and spoke words of love and
counsel. She told Evelina that she should hang the
painting in the study-room, — not to cause her useless pain, but because she hoped the sight of it
would be a constant lesson, and exert a salutary
influence. Evelina received this information with
the same stolid indifference. Miss Newton went
away, hoping she had sown some seed on good
ground. Alas! it was not good, but stony.

It was in the middle of the afternoon session before the principal teacher once more took her place
at the desk. Her face was grave, but a half smile
of loving-kindness always played with the firm lines
around her mouth.

The picture was hung upon the wall. No stranger could have seen aught in it, save a work of

great merit and beauty; but to them it spoke vo-
lumes of human love and passion. Miss Newton
did not let this opportunity pass without reminding
the girls, in her own quiet way, of their duties to
each other, and the necessity of that charity "which
suffereth long and is kind."

CHAPTER XI

THE TRUE POET.

As the last book disappeared in Alice's desk at the close of the session, her seat-mate, Ellen, bent towards her, and asked her if she would not like to walk home with her. It was a warm day in the later summer, and Alice readily consented, and said she should be only too happy to go. "Let's go 'cross-lots,'" said Ellen; "for I want to talk to you, and I don't want to meet any one."

They walked on some distance in silence. Ellen seemed troubled, and Alice waited for her to begin the conversation. By going across the meadows they avoided the dusty road. The field-grass rose up to kiss their feet; the great trees threw their cooling shadows across the path; and the low, plaintive tinkling of the cow-bell sounded in the distance. Beyond the valley the church reared its white front; and its vane caught the slant sunbeams like a halo of glory. Alice was a child of nature: every bird and flower and sun-ray seemed to her so many links of that great chain which is ever drawing us nearer to heaven and God. "O God! I thank thee for this beautiful life!" was the silent thanksgiving of her heart.

A low sob fell upon her ear; and, looking up, she saw that Ellen was weeping.

" I am afraid you think I am gloomy, Alice," said she ; " but I have been sad all day. I wish I could be cheerful and happy as you are."

" That is because you looked on the ground, and I looked up at the beautiful sunshine and the blue sky."

" That will do for those who are rich and happy," said Ellen. " Suppose you were poor, Alice, and all your hopeful future hedged about with difficulties ? "

" But I have been poor," said Alice. " My mother was a widow, much poorer than yours, and I am only a poor orphan now, and mean to earn my own bread sometime. But what difficulties have you ? Has any thing happened ? "

" No : only I feel just so. And I don't see any hope of my ever being anybody. I suppose I am ungrateful ; for Miss Newton told me only to-day that she had engaged a school for me, when I have finished my studies."

" Why, Ellen Lee ! How can you be sad over that news ! If it was me, I should be happy for a week."

" And so was I when I first heard it ; but I'm afraid it won't do me much good ! I shouldn't wonder if I had to leave school, Alice. Mother's health is so feeble, that it really makes my heart

ache to leave her in the morning. Much as I want
to teach, I believe I shall give it up; for I can't
see her kill herself."

"But can't something be done?" said Alice.
"It is a pity to give it up, with the battle half
fought."

. "No," said Ellen despondingly; "there's no
help for it."

"And then again," said Ellen, "I don't know
as I should be contented to teach, if I could as well
as not. The fact is, I don't think I am fitted for it;
there is too much cold practicability about it. I
like the ideal, the sunny, the imaginative. In truth,
Alice, I believe my true path lies in the walks of
literature. If I could be a writer, I should be
satisfied."

"But it plainly would not be your duty," said
Alice.

"Why not, pray?"

"Because, do you not see that your mother looks
forward to you to aid her, and labors to place you
where you can gain a livelihood? If you were
rich, it would be well enough; but as it is, without
money, without literary friends, it would be a long
time before you could support yourself with your
pen."

"I know it," replied Ellen; "and that's just·
what I'm finding fault about. Because I am poor,
I must deny myself, when I would work; but the

rich can revel in idleness. Where is the justice of this?"

"Our lives are in the hands of our Maker," said Alice. "Perhaps he sees you need the discipline of trial. Walk in the path of duty, and wait patiently."

"And is it my duty? Is it my duty to crush all these glowing aspirations, to give up the true beauty, the breathing joy of poetry, for a cold reality? Must I live all my life long like Tantalus; for ever reaching for golden fruits and cooling water, and continually denied? Say, Alice, can this be my duty?"

"No, my dear friend, it is not your duty to give up all these; but it is your duty, under present circumstances, to live your poetry instead of writing it."

"Live my poetry, Alice? Pray explain."

"The sweetest poems, Ellen, are those which are unwritten. You will find them in living characters, in the lines which furrow the brows of suffering women; you will read them in the white locks of toil-spent men. The brightest epic is a life of self-sacrifice, and the sweetest lyric a lifetime of love."

"But there are enough in the world," said Ellen, "who will not work. Dull plodders, who have no aspirations above the level of the actual."

"Not so, my friend. 'Labor,' says Carlyle, 'is the essence of all heroism.' We have no right to lay our burdens on the shoulders of others."

" Here we are," said Ellen, " at the half-way stone. Let us sit down. I believe, Alice, you are my good angel; for you always encourage me with some higher view of life. I wish I were as strong as you. Will you tell me your idea of a true poet ? "

" The true poet," said Alice, " is, to me, a great soul, capable at once of high aspirations and simple affections. The inner world is his home, and he can read the mysteries of the veiled heart. One need not necessarily write to be a poet. Poetry is Love, and Love is God ; so he that loves becomes like God, and is a poet. He who loves his brother, and helps humanity everywhere ; who chooses the path of duty, whether rough or flowery, and walks in it thanking God, — he is a poet."

" I can see, Alice," said Ellen, " that you mean to tell me my duty. Well, I need it. I confess I have felt envious of others, that I have grumbled at the occupations which I deemed menial. When I milked the cow, or washed the dishes, I have thought of the jewelled hands of my schoolmates, and murmured at my lot. Henceforth, I will try to live a little poetry."

There was another silence, which Alice finally broke by asking Ellen what situation Miss Newton had secured for her.

" It is a vacancy in the Graham Institute. I am to teach Botany and Rhetoric, my favorite branches you know. But then," and the old sadness came back to her face, " how I am going to keep at school I don't know. Mother must have help, or she will die."

" You must throw off despondency, and work. If I could contrive a way to help you, would you accept my aid ? "

" Any thing from you, dear Alice ! you are so good. How I wish I were like you, a blessing to every one ! "

Alice put her hand on Ellen's lips, and said, — " Goodby now : you will be better in the morning ; and perhaps I shall have something to tell you."

A new idea had entered Alice's mind ; and she proceeded to act upon it.

CHAPTER XII

WITH a light and happy heart, Alice crossed the meadow, climbed over the huge stepping-stones, and entered the road. She was happy, because she was bound on a mission of benevolence. So absorbed was she in her own thoughts, that she did not hear light footsteps behind her, till a childish voice exclaimed, "Oh! is it you, Miss Alice? I am so glad to see you!"

Alice turned round. A pretty child, with rosy cheeks, stood before her. Her bonnet had partly fallen from her head. One plump hand held a basket, filled with flowers and mosses; while with the other she held back her dog, who was trying to show his joy by leaping on Alice with his great paws.

"Down, Bouncer! Haven't you any manners? You must excuse him, Miss Alice; for I really don't think he knows any better. Father says he thinks some dogs have souls. Do you, Miss Alice?"

"I don't know, Nina. You must ask them."

"But they can't speak!"

"And consequently," said Alice, "we shall never know whether they have souls or not. But where have you been this afternoon, Nina?"

"Oh! I went down to the brook to see Edward

fish. But I felt so bad to see the pretty trout flapping on that dreadful hook, that I went over the hill to get some mosses for my castle. See! aren't they pretty?" and the child drew up the bright green mosses from her basket. '

" They are very pretty, Nina. But where is your castle?"

"Oh! I'm building it at the foot of the apple-tree in the orchard. I've made it out of gray bark; and this moss will fill up the cracks."

" I'm going down to your house now," said Alice, " and I can stop and see it."

"Oh, I'm so glad!" cried Nina delightedly. "Then, perhaps, you will tell me how to make the loopholes. Brother Edward said I must have some. Did you know my brother Edward had come home, Alice?"

" Yes; and I suppose you are glad, are you not?"

" Oh, yes!" said the child. " And he likes you; for he asked father who that young lady was that sat opposite our pew on Sunday, and I told him it was my sabbath teacher, and I loved her very much. He said he thought he should too. Isn't he a funny brother, Alice?"

" You mustn't speak of these things, Nina. Your brother did not mean that you should tell any one."

Judge Hall's splendid residence was surrounded with extensive grounds. A broad avenue led to the house; and the tall elms stretched their shadows across the lawn. As they opened the gate, little Freddy, the youngest child, ran to meet them; for he had seen Alice much, and learned to love her.

"Won't you come and look at my castle?" said Nina.

"No, not now," replied Alice. "I want to see your father."

Alice's ring was answered by a noble-looking young man, who invited her into the parlor. "My father is occupied just at present," said he, "but will be in soon." He introduced himself with graceful ease,— spoke of books, and foreign travel; but Alice could not help remembering Nina's words, and she felt uncomfortable. He had spent three years at the German Law School at Heidelberg; and had come back a polished and thoroughly educated man. Much as Alice enjoyed his conversation, she felt relieved when Judge Hall came in and his son retired.

The judge was a corpulent, good-natured man. His cheeks were as red as the rosy side of a winter's apple; and his eyes were blue, the very color of virtue.

Alice was a general favorite in the family,— from the judge, who always expressed vast partiality for her, down to little Freddy, who remembered the paper boats she had built for him, and the kites she knew so well how to make.

"Well, Miss Morton," said he, "you must excuse me, but some law-papers detained me. I am truly glad to see you!"

"Thank you," said Alice. "I came to lay a proposition before you, if you will be troubled with it."

The judge signified his willingness to be troubled.

"You know Ellen Lee, do you not?" said Alice.

"What, — the Widow Lee's daughter? Yes; and she is a fine girl, — the finest I know except one."

Alice would not notice the sly hint, but continued: "Ellen's mother supports herself by her needle; and, now her son is away, she finds it hard work to live. Ellen is very ambitious, and wishes to be a teacher. She has a situation already offered her, in case she finishes her studies, — for she is the best scholar in the seminary; but her mother's health is so poor, that, unless she can have aid, Ellen will have to leave school altogether."

"How much would she need?" interrupted the judge.

"Oh! they never would accept charity, were it never so delicate. I think I have a better way, if you approve it. I think you told me some time ago that you would like to get some one to give Nina and Freddy single lessons, did you not?"

"I did think some of it," replied he.

"Then, if you do wish such a one, let me beg you to employ Ellen Lee. It would be doing a good deed. She has an hour and a half at noon, which she could devote to this; and it would help her so much!"

Alice's whole heart was in the work, and she was unconscious of the earnestness of her manner.

"I declare," said the judge admiringly, "you'd make an extra pleader. I believe I shall surrender at discretion."

"And may I tell Ellen to come?" said Alice, blushing.

"Yes: upon the whole, I guess you may," said the judge. "If she can manage the children, it will be a good thing for them."

"Thank you, thank you!" said Alice. "I was afraid you had engaged some one else. Ellen will be so happy!"

"But why did she not come herself?" inquired the judge.

"She knows nothing about it," replied Alice. "She was telling me of her troubles, and I thought perhaps you might be willing to help her. It will be a very pleasant surprise to her."

"Well, you may tell her to come to-morrow noon, and I will see her. And now what shall I do for you, Miss Alice?"

"You will please receive my thanks for your kind favor," said Alice.

"But do you never think of yourself, child?"

"Oh, yes! Mr. Hall; I am selfish in many ways. I am very exacting about the love of my friends. If I do any thing for them, I want a great deal of love in payment. I have not yet learned to give, hoping for nothing again."

Alice rose to go.

" I am a blunt man," said the judge, "and my life has lost its morning flush. I cannot trust men as I did once; but I believe the Lord made an angel when he made you. May he keep your heart from every shadow of trial!"

" I thank you," said Alice ; " but I pray not so. Ask him rather to afflict me as he seeth good ; for, without the discipline of sorrow, the soul may never know its strength, or unfold its wings."

" A strange girl, and too thoughtful," said the judge to himself.

Edward Hall sat upon the piazza as she passed out, and begged so politely to attend her to the seminary, that she could not refuse.

" I think it is perfectly scandalous," said Evelina Cobb, who was peeping through the blinds, when Edward took leave of Alice at the gate.

" I always said there was mischief under all that girl's sanctimonious manners," said Jane Swift.

" Truly, ' there is that maketh himself poor, yet hath great riches,'" said the judge to himself, as he sat in his library that night.

" What did you say, father," said Edward.

" I was thinking of Alice Morton," said his father " She is a poor orphan ; but the wealth of her mind

5

and heart is inexhaustible. Happy they who are favored with her self-forgetting friendship."

' "I think her a true lady," said his son. "I have not met with such great dignity and modesty among the most polished women of Europe."

CHAPTER XIII

"IT is impossible, Emily," said Mr. Whiting, as he rose to go. "I cannot spare the money to-day."

"But it is only five hundred dollars," said the lady fretfully, as she balanced her spoon on the edge of her cup. "Lizzie has set her heart on wearing those ornaments to-morrow night. It wouldn't hurt you to gratify the child in such a trifle."

"But it would hurt me," said her husband. "I have a heavy note to pay to-day, and it will require all my means to meet it. Next week, perhaps, I could let you have it."

"Just a week too late," said the lady pettishly. "For my part, I don't think you need to refuse. You don't think any thing of paying out a large sum of money when the girls' school-bills come in, and you always settle Fred's enormous accounts without a word. And you can pay two hundred dollars for a gold watch for Alice ; but, when your own daughter asks a favor, she must be denied."

Mr. Whiting's brow clouded. "I have always tried to satisfy every reasonable desire," said he ; "but I have told you why I cannot meet this demand. As for the girls' school-bills, they shall be paid as long as I have a cent. They are buying what is worth far more than jewels, — education and character."

"A vast sight of good their school will do them!" said his wife. "They will come back as prim as old maids, and as awkward as bean-poles."

"Better so," was the reply, "than to be fashionable flirts;" and, thus saying, Mr. Whiting took his hat from the hall, and left the house.

The lady still balanced her spoon on the edge of her cup, and drummed the carpet with her foot; while her vexation grew stronger every minute. The chocolate was cooling, and the toast was cold; and still Lizzie had not made her appearance at the breakfast-table. Mrs. Whiting pulled the bell, and sent for her. No morning greetings passed between the mother and her stylish daughter; but Lizzie's first inquiry was, "Well, mother, what did pa say about the jewels?"

"Perhaps, after all, it would be as well for you to wear your pearls to-morrow night," said her mother, when she had explained.

"I won't do any such thing," said Lizzie; "I've worn those pearls till I'm tired of the sight of them. Louis Melville will be there, and I won't have Isabella Howard outdo me."

Mrs. Whiting declared that such things always gave her a dreadful headache, and retired to her room.

"I will have them," said Lizzie, as she rose from her chair, and placed her foot firmly upon the floor. "If begging won't bring them, perhaps teasing will. Father never refused me any thing yet, and I don't believe he will now."

The cloud was still upon Mr. Whiting's brow as he sat down to dinner. Lizzie was very pleasant and thoughtful,—for she could be good-natured when it suited her convenience. The unwonted kindness of his daughter lifted the shadow somewhat from the face of her too indulgent father; for he did not suspect that she was selfish, even in her kindness. In truth, he had almost forgotten the morning's scene, in his business troubles. The failure of a heavy firm which was indebted to him had rendered it very difficult for him to meet his payments."

"Father," said Lizzie, as he pushed his chair away from his almost untasted dinner, "wont you please buy me those jewels?"

The cloud settled again upon her father's face.

"I cannot to-day, Lizzie. Would you have them at the risk of your father's credit?"

"I don't see how five hundred dollars can affect a wealthy man like you. Other girls have every thing they want, and I don't see why I cant."

"Lizzie, listen to me," said her father. "I will explain the whole matter to you, and then if you still desire the jewels you shall have them. I have

confidence enough in your judgment; and I throw
the decision entirely on your good sense. There is
a heavy firm out West," continued he, " who have
recently failed. I held a note of theirs for a large
sum, and I was depending on this to meet my own
regular payments. Others have suffered from the
same cause, so that a general pressure is felt among
business men. Those who can pass this crisis and
redeem their notes at the bank will come out doubly
strong; but those who cannot will find their credit
shaken. Now, this money which you want may possibly help me a great deal. If money is easy, I can
stand without difficulty; but, if not, this five hundred dollars might supply the very deficiency in
point. Now I am sure, Lizzie, you will answer
like a true-minded girl. Let my daughter respect
herself, and let the foolish fancy go."

Mr. Whiting's mild blue eyes were fixed upon
his daughter's face; but Lizzie never looked up, but
kept on tracing out the figure on the carpet with her
foot. He thought, perhaps, it would be well to
leave her alone, that she might not decide hastily.

"Lizzie," said he, "I am going out a few moments. I shall expect your answer when I return.
Remember that I never refused you any thing that I
could rightly give; and think, also, how much depends on your decision."

Mr. Whiting did not once doubt that Lizzie would
be true to her better nature. He did not know that

the root of selfishness and the fibres of vanity strike deeper even than duty or filial love.

Lizzie rose from the table, and went to the glass. "It is too bad!" said she, as she smoothed back her hair from her temples; "those jewels would just suit my style. I don't believe he would know the difference in a month. And then Isabella Howard says that all fathers are alike. They are always pleading poverty. Yes, yes, I must have them!" she repeated to herself. "I *will* have them. I can't help it if it is wrong," she replied, to the faint whisper of her stifled conscience. "Louis Melville will be there, and I must have them!"

Mr. Whiting's step sounded in the hall, and every footfall made Lizzie's heart beat faster. She felt that she was about to degrade herself, and disappoint him.

"Well, Lizzie?"

"I wish — that is, I thought, — I have decided to have the jewels," she faltered, with her eyes still fixed upon the carpet. She dared not look up to meet the reproach she knew was in his gaze.

"My daughter!" What a world of tender sadness, of disappointed love, was in those words! Silently, and with a strange heaviness of heart, he left her there, and closed the street-door behind him.

That afternoon saw Lizzie Whiting the possessor of the coveted jewels; but the memory of that sad

voice seemed to rob them of half their lustre.   Her
fashionable mother praised her tact, and said she had
managed it finely.   Her young lady friends flattered and envied her, and that was all.

But was it all?

That afternoon saw Mr. Whiting weary and discouraged.   With his utmost endeavors, he still
lacked somewhat of the sum required.   His paper
had never been dishonored, and the very thought
was madness.   He was obliged to do what he never
had done before, — borrow money at a ruinous interest to save his credit at the bank.

And this was all.   But was it all?   Was it nothing that a father's faith in his child was shaken?
was it nothing that the daughter, whose father's fond
indulgence should have met the reward of sympathy
and love, had given him back only a selfish ingrati-
tude?   It is true that the money might not have
saved Mr. Whiting from his embarrassments ; but,
oh! how the memory of a fond child's loving self-
sacrifice would have lightened the heavy heart he
bore home with him that night!

Who shall blame him if bitter thoughts were in
his mind?   It was just dusk, and the laborers were
going home with light hearts from their work.   Mr.
Whiting thought of the homely hearths made plea--
sant for them by household mirth and childish
laughter ; and then, turning the picture, he saw his
own cheerless rooms, where even the sunlight could

not penetrate, lest it should fade the velvet furniture
and costly carpets.   Even love and tenderness were
banished, because they were too common and un-
genteel.   Fashion and folly had plucked all the
sweet fruits of his life, and thrown him the empty
husks.

Mr. Whiting ate his supper from a service of the
finest of Sevres china; but, for all that, his heart
was heavy, and he would gladly have exchanged it
for the poor laborer's earthen bowl, for but a tithe of
the aid and sympathy he received.   How rich, and
yet how poor!   Splendid misery at home, — a cold
world beyond!   A nervous, gloomy wife at home,
— a smiling, fashionable wife in society!   A selfish,
vain daughter at home, — a gay, beautiful belle in
society!   What was life to him, but an empty
gilding?

. He took out his letters, and singled out one with
a dainty white envelope: it was from Alice,
and was filled with words of gratitude and affection.
And, what was best, he knew that it was not mere
lip-service.   He remembered how many times the
ready hands had done him service; and how
many times the sweet voice had said, " Dear Uncle
William! "   Alice had sent her best love to black
John, and asked Uncle William to tell Content that
she had bought a bright bandanna to give her when
she came home.

Mr. Whiting had been restless and uneasy all the
5*

evening.   His wife and daughter were away, and
the great rooms seemed desolate.   " I have a great
mind," he said to himself, " to go into the kitchen
and see John and Content."   So he passed through
the long passage, and knocked at the door.

Content opened it.

" Lor' bress us, Massa Whiting ! — am any thing
de matter ? "

" No, Content!   I've only come to see you."   ⸱

" Thank ye," said she, dropping a short courtesy,
and brushing the bottom of a chair vigorously with her
apron.   " Ole John just done been reading.   Better
stop now," she added, in a loud whisper to John.

" No, no ! — go on," said Mr. Whiting.

John read in his broken way, — with his finger
pointing to the words as he spoke, — " There is
that maketh himself rich, yet hath nothing ; there is
that maketh himself poor, yet hath great riches."

Mr. Whiting listened, half in awe.   It seemed
like a voice from heaven.   The proud man felt
humbled before a poor unlettered black.   He did
not like to think of it, but told John he had better
put away the book, as he had something to tell
them ; and then he delivered Alice's message.

The tears stood in John's eyes, and he said
nothing ; but Content was loud in her joy.

" May de good Lor' bress de dear chile ! " said
she.   " He done make her an angel already ! "

Mr. Whiting thought perhaps she was right.

CHAPTER XIV

THE HUSKING.

" Won't it be splendid, girls ? " exclaimed Emma Weston, as she bounded into the school-room. " Judge Hall is going to give a husking party next Friday night, and we're all invited."

" I don't think it is just fit work for young ladies," said the nice Lucy Howard.

" Nor I either," said some others; " but we always have such a good time at the judge's."

The autumn had come, and thrown its gold and purple glory over the forests and hill-sides. The brown nuts dropped in the woods, the grey squirrels were providing for the winter, and the evening cricket sang a shriller melody in the grass. It was the joyous harvest-time, — the season of New England merry-making. The apples were gathered in the orchards ; and the fields were bare and desolate, save where some golden pumpkin turned its cheek to the noonday sun.

Judge Hall was a New-Englander of the good old stock, and he delighted in reviving the customs of our forefathers. He believed in Thanksgiving cheer, and subscribed to Christmas apples, cider, and chicken pies ; and never a year passed that he did not invite the youth of the village to a famous husking.

Friday evening came, and the girls, one by one, gathered in the dressing-room, ready for departure.

"Alice! Alice! where are you?" The voice was loud and petulant.

"Here I am, Cousin Ada; but please don't make so much noise, for Lily's head aches badly."

. "Come," said Ada, — "here we've been hunting for you half an hour, and you're not ready yet. I declare," said she, "its enough to provoke a saint! Here you are plodding round, and not even dressed. You grow more and more old-maidish every day."

"Please, cousin, don't make so much noise," said Alice pleadingly. "I'm afraid that Lily is really sick."

Lily lay hot and feverish. Her brow was heated and flushed. Ada thought perhaps she might be sick, after all.

"I believe I ought not to go," said Alice.

"Oh, yes! go by all means," said Lily; "I wouldn't deprive you of so much pleasure. I suspect it is nothing more than a cold. I sat by the window last night, and my lungs feel very much oppressed. You couldn't do me any good if you stay; for I shall retire immediately, and try to sleep it off."

"As true as I live, I haven't got any thing decent to wear," said Evelina Cobb, as she pulled dress after dress out of her trunk.

"Why don't you wear your new muslin?" ventured Jane Swift.

"Horror! I wouldn't be seen with it. It isn't an evening dress. On the whole, I believe I'll wear my pink silk." So the old pink silk was brought up from the bottom of the trunk, where it had lain waiting, as Evelina had before said, till she should be invited to some ball. Jane ventured to suggest that she didn't think it was just suitable to husk corn in; but Evelina declared she had no doubt there would be many city people there, and she wanted them to know she was somebody.

"I know the true reason why you are so particular," said Jane. "Edward Hall will be there. But you don't stand any chance if Alice Morton goes, for they say he adores her."

"*They* say! Who says?"

"Why, — they, of course. Not any one in particular, — *they*."

The harvest moon hung low in the sky as the two girls left the seminary. Beyond the brow of the hill, they could see the windows of the judge's house brilliantly illuminated; and the sound of music and festivity came to their ears.

Little Nina stood at the head of the stairs as the young ladies passed in.

"Has Miss Ellen come? I want to see Miss Ellen."

Ellen came forward to speak to her little pupil.

Nina's spirits were exuberant, and she could hardly command her tongue to tell her teacher that her father wished to see her in the library.

"What can it be?" thought Ellen, half in consternation. She could think of no neglected duty, and concluded to put an end to suspense by answering the call immediately.

The great barns were hung with lanterns, and the corn was thrown in great heaps on the floor. The girls quickly appropriated the stools, and commenced the novel work with a good will. Some kind hand seemed to have plentifully sprinkled the heaps with red ears, and much confusion and many kisses was the result.

It was a pretty scene. Bright faces were radiant with smiles; nimble fingers robbed the golden ears of their rough coats; and music and lively talk made every thing cheerful and happy. It made Alice think of her own home, and brought to her mind the pleasant huskings and apple-gatherings of long ago. To most of the girls, however, it was a new scene; and they seemed to enjoy it highly. Alice would have been very happy, had not the thought of Lily saddened her; and she almost blamed herself for coming.

"Miss Lee," said Edward, addressing Ellen, "can you tell me who that girl is, standing by Miss Morton?"

"That is Evelina Cobb," replied Ellen.

"What a contrast!" ejaculated her companion. And well he might say so. Evelina's showy dress and simpering airs appeared in all their deformity, beside Alice's neat dress and simple manners.

Towards the latter part of the evening, Ellen drew Alice aside, and told her of her interview with the judge. It seemed that he had interested himself for Charles, and, by his influence, induced other gentlemen to acknowledge his talents, and give him employment. And now these gentlemen, patrons of art, and eager to encourage home genius, wished to send him to Europe to finish his studies; while he copied famous pictures by their order.

"It is owing to you, indirectly," said Ellen; "for, if I had not come here to teach, the judge would not have so interested himself for Charles. How shall I ever thank you?"

"By saying nothing about such a poor little favor. But do you think your mother will be willing to have him go?"

"Oh, yes! I think she will. Of course, it will cause her much anxiety; but then she knows it has always been a cherished hope of Charles, that he might some day walk the soil hallowed by the tread of the world's great painters, and drink a new inspiration from the very fountain-head of art. O Alice! it is a glorious thought! I wish I might once breathe that air; sanctified by ages of song, and deified by the very essence of heroism and poesy." Carried away by her enthusiasm, Ellen was unconscious of the company, and unmindful that curious eyes might be upon her. Her eyes glowed with impassioned fire, her hand was raised, in the force of her feelings; and she stood for the moment like a speaking muse, pleading the cause she loved.

Alice was moved. She acknowledged the power, the genius of her companion; but her feelings were under the control of reason and duty. Not that she could not be enthusiastic, not that poetry and passion had no inspiration for her; but because Reason told her that constant longing after things beyond our reach was both a weakness and a breach of duty, when so much of good lay unwrought at our very feet.

There is no being so inquisitive as the student of character. Edward Hall was one of these. He delighted to trace in the workings of the face, and in the conversation of those about him, the peculiar motives which give a bias to the mind, and a form to the daily life. All this evening, he had wandered from group to group, drawing out this one, and studying another, and had been an involuntary listener to our friends' conversation.

"I do wish, Ellen," said Alice, " that circumstances favored your wishes; but you must control yourself. Gifts never came by the mere wishing; and Italy never will come to you. If your whole soul is bent on this end, you will accomplish it; but you must give up rhapsodies, and expend that nervous energy in working for your object, instead of a mere effervesence. But I do hope, my dear friend," — and Alice's voice sank to a deeper tone, — "that life has some higher aim for you than a mere vision of the land of song. The ends of our existence are only met when a noble labor sanctifies life as a means to the great Hereafter, the infinite Progression. Let your genius be a gift upon the altar, — a constant incense from a pure heart; so that you may say at last, 'I have fought a good fight, I have kept the faith, I have finished my course. Henceforth there is laid up for me a crown of glory.'"

"Quoting Scripture, as I live," said Lucy Howard, as she passed by them. The last place, I should think, for that."

But Ellen was unmindful of all. A new idea had occurred to her, and she grasped it.

"Do you believe, Alice," she said, "do you *know* that we *can* do what we *will* do?"

"I believe it firmly," said Alice, "if we have decision and energy."

"Then," said Ellen, "if I live, I will go to Italy."

Alice linked her arm in Ellen's, and walked away. Just then a profusion of flaxen hair and a pair of cold blue eyes intercepted Edward's vision, and a loud voice exclaimed, "Good evening, Mr. Hall!"

" Good evening, Miss Cobb," said Edward coldly.

" What a beautiful entertainment you have made here ! " said Evelina. " I never attended a husking before, and I'm perfectly enchanted."

Edward smiled to himself, as he remembered having heard her declare to Ada that she thought it was one of the meanest affairs she ever saw, and not decent for genteel people."

" Miss Cobb," said he, " I am a student of law ; and the question has come up to me this evening, whether, if a person testifies ' yes ' and ' no ' on the same subject, his word should be taken as reliable. Excuse me, but I would like to know what you think about it."

Evelina, who did not see the hidden sarcasm in his words, felt flattered, and answered, —

" I don't know much about ' law,' but I should think not."

Edward replied by reciting a couplet he had composed the year before : —

" The double tongue is like the double face,
    Alike a condemnation and disgrace."

" Oh, yes ! " said Evelina, " I remember those lines very well. I have read Byron so much, that I know him all by heart. Do you like Byron, Mr. Hall ! "

Edward saw the shallowness of the stream he was fording, and thought he might venture a little deeper.

" Yes," he continued, " Byron will do very well. Are you fond of poetry ? "

Oh ! excessively. Poetry is one of the fine arts. How thankful we ought to be to those who invented it ! "

" We ought, indeed," said Edward, with profound gravity. " Your remarks are just. Poetry is a great discovery, and will go down to posterity hand in hand with the invention of gunpowder and the printing-press. But I believe the world disputes about the author of the invention. Pray, what is your opinion, Miss Cobb ? "

Edward was interested. He had truly found an interesting study; while his poor victim believed the very pain he meant but a pleasure and a triumph.

" I think it was got up in Greece," she answered. " They were quite skilful, I believe, in putting words together."

Edward was delighted with his success. " Oh, yes ! " he continued, " it was a perfectly mechanical thing. If legends speak correctly, they managed it in this way. In those days they had no railroad : but they had a sort of telegraph between the earth and Mount Parnassus, by which the poets could send up requests, and the muses return an answer. So, when one of the old bards wanted to write a poem, he just sent up a message on this ' thread of discourse,' and they sent back the needed words.

It was very much like setting types. Excuse me," said he, as he noticed that one of his friends was nearly choking with mirth,—"allow me, Miss Cobb, to introduce to you Mr. White." Mr. White forced back the laugh with a great effort, and the fun-loving Edward left them to continue the conversation he had broken so abruptly.

"It is too bad, Edward," said a friend who stood by him. "You were not only rude, but positively unkind."

"My dear friend," said Edward, "what sent that dark trouble into your blue eyes? Don't you know, that, where people have no sensibilities, they cannot be blunted? And, when I see folly and pretension passing current among those of real worth, I make it a point to unmask and expose it."

The night was warm and cloudless. A walk through the grounds was proposed, and many eagerly rose to respond to the call. Edward was conscious that many eyes were upon him; but he passed by the gay dresses and jewelled hands, and, seeking out Alice, begged leave to accompany her.

The harvest moon still threw its silver glory over the quiet earth; the dew sparkled in the grass like lost crystals; and the air was still and waveless, as though it said, "Hush!"

"Would," said Edward, "that our lives might flow as calmly into the great future! What is the use of living? what is the use of striving? There is no certainty save death. Miss Morton ". said he, with a sudden energy, "do you believe in love and in faith?"

With a half-timid glance, as if she feared a negative, she answered, "Yes: do not you?"

"Yes," he replied, "I do; but I wanted, to strengthen my belief by hearing an avowal of yours. After all, the simple trust of one loving spirit is worth more than all the philosophies of men. Germany is a poor place in which to learn faith, Miss Morton."

Alice said she hoped the theories of dreamers had not shaken his trust in his fathers' God.

"You are severe," he replied. "There is something in this you style ' theory,' which, I confess, holds me as my fathers' faith never did."

"I was none too severe, I think. It is because these dreams of the German mystics lead youth astray from active faith and duty, that I so much dread their influence. They fasten on the mind while it is not strong enough to resist, and shipwreck faith on the rocks of a barren philosophy."

Edward looked at her in surprise. "Pray, where did you learn all this?"

Alice smiled. "I have read German somewhat; and this peculiar form of thought appears so plainly in every thing they write, that I could not avoid a knowledge of it, even if I would."

"And you disapprove it?" continued her companion. "But all things are mysterious,—no one has told us concerning a future life."

"A divine voice whispers to us," said Alice,—"'The kingdom of heaven is within you.'"

Edward was silent for some time : at last he said, "I confess I have given these ideas too much scope. Will you teach me faith, Miss Morton? I could not fail to be an apt scholar under your instruction."

Once more Alice smiled,—the same old quiet smile. Edward noticed it.

"You think me childish?" said he.

"No! oh, no!" said Alice. "I was only thinking how strange it was, that you, who have sat at the feet of the world's teachers and divines, and felt the very droppings of wisdom ; and, more than all, lived for so many years in the light of God's love and blessing,— that you, I say, should come to me and ask for faith. It is a paradox. I am a child in argument, Mr. Hall."

"And, therefore, 'the greatest in the kingdom of heaven,'" was the reply. "I will confess to you that there are times when all the lore of the schools is folly to me ; and I could throw myself at the feet of a loving disciple like you and learn the alphabet. I was fortunate enough to hear your recent conversation with Miss Lee. I am proud of my countrywomen. Their sound good sense is the safeguard of the American people."

They walked slowly back to the house. The

barns were deserted; but a bountiful entertainment awaited the guests in the dining-room. Judge Hall literally carried out the old New England customs. No cakes or ices met their view; but huge turkeys, cold meats, and pies occupied their places, to the astonishment of "eyes polite."

The light burned dimly in the chamber as Alice entered it after her return from the party. A quick cry of alarm escaped her lips as she saw Lily's flushed cheeks, and listened to her delirious words. She still lay as she had thrown herself down in her tight dress. Very tenderly Alice undressed her, smoothed the pillow, and tried to calm her excited mind; but Lily did not recognize her.

"I wonder where Alice is!" she would say. "I wish Alice would come! They have left me alone."

"No, Lily; here I am, — here is Alice. Dear, dear Lily, don't you know me?" pleaded Alice.

"No, I don't know any of it. *J'ai, tu as, il a,*" — she muttered. "I can't recite it. Alice used to love me once, — go away, and let Alice come."

Alice reproached herself over and over again for leaving her. She smoothed the pillow once more, and bathed the poor girl's head. The cooling drops seemed to calm her.

With sudden hope springing up in her heart, Alice leaned forward. "You know me now, dear Lily?"

A smile flitted over her face. "Mother!" she said, and sank into a broken slumber.

CHAPTER XV.

THE FADED FLOWER.

THE closing of a young life is like the closing of a flower. As the delicate petals fold over its heart when the darkness is abroad, and the chill night-winds blow, so the eyelids close to all the gloom and vain glories of this earth. Happy that spirit which, like the flower, has sent up its best fragrance for Heaven, and kept its holiest shrine pure and un-spotted from the world. So pure, so calm and holy, is death to the earnest soul. As the flower closes at night to open again in the broad light of to-morrow's sun, so our human blossoms shut their weary eyelids upon "the valley of the shadow," to open the eyelids of the spirit in the blessed "mansions of our Father's house."

Lily was dying. Loving hearts could no longer deceive themselves with a hope. Day by day they watched her growing paler and thinner, as the crimson flush of fever abated. The fire was going out on the hearth of life. The delirium had passed; and she lay in a dreamy exhaustion, as if, half-disen-thralled, she had caught a glimpse of the inner glory.

A hush settled over the school, and loud voices and bounding footsteps died into a softened murmur as they passed the door of the sick room. They knew that there Death and Life played a fearful game of shuttlecock, and that Death had almost won.

It was the afternoon of a clear October day. Lily lay propped up by pillows, — her cheek blanched by suffering, but patient, as she always was. The doctor had just been encouraging her by cheering words ; but for an answer Lily only shook her head, and pointed upward. Mrs. Cushing had been early called to the bedside of her child, and she had watched and prayed as none but an idolizing mother can. Rising, and following the doctor to the door, she exclaimed, "Doctor! cannot you give me some hope? oh! I pray you — I implore you — give me some hope!" "While there is life there is hope," he answered. "Which means you have none," said Mrs. Cushing, in a voice of despair. "Oh, my Father! my punishment is greater than I can bear!"

The good doctor turned round, that she might not perceive the unusual moisture in his eyes. "Whom the Lord loveth he chasteneth," said he.

"Yes : I am an alien from Him. I disobeyed the command, 'Little children, keep yourselves from idols.' But, oh! I cannot give her up, doctor! I cannot! Will he break the bruised reed?"

The agony of the appeal, the grief of the heart-stricken mother, were too much for the good man's philosophy ; he felt the tears coming, and, hastily pressing her hand, bade her "good-day," and de-

6

parted. When he had gone, Mrs. Cushing sat down in the upper hall, and gave way to her grief.

The flood, long pent up, will burst forth at last. Then she calmed herself, prayed earnestly for strength, and went back to the bedside of her departing child.

Alice sat by her, engaged in earnest conversation. Lily never tired of her; for Alice's sound, practical piety and Christian hope were just what her fainting soul needed. Alice had been talking to her of heaven, of the " Good Shepherd's " love. Mrs. Cushing paused on the threshold, as she caught a vision of Lily's saint-like countenance. A look of holy joy beamed like a dawning light upon her face : her mother clasped her hands involuntarily, as if to hold a treasure that was escaping from her. " You have been weeping, mother," said she; " oh! why will you distress yourself? Do you not see that I am happy? Dear mother! I love you so much! Shall you be very sorry when I am gone ? "

The old rushing flood in the mother's heart rose up again, and overflowed her eyes. Her only reply was a shower of passionate kisses. " Listen, mother," said Lily : " Alice has been telling me of the angels, of their purity and love; and, as I listened, her voice, so soft and low, seemed to me like the rustling of their wings; and her eyes did not seem like Alice's, but like a spirit's, mild and earnest, looking down upon me full of divine pity. I am a poor,

weak, human child, and I forgot Alice; and her low
talking seemed to me like the words of my angel-
friend, and I thought I was in heaven. I will come
for you when the sun is setting," said she, "for the
gates of heaven open wider, and let out a whole
flood of glory; I will come for you then, and you
shall pass directly in at the portals. Watch and
pray. Behold! I come quickly." The tears rained
over the mother's face; it seemed as though the
mournful affliction were really come. "I believe
she will come, mother," repeated Lily, "and I want
to talk to you now while I can. When I am gone
to heaven you will be very lonely: there will be no
voice to say 'mother,' no daughter to pray for; the
books in my little library will be unread, and my
harp will be silent. This must not be. You must
have another daughter to take my place. I love
Alice as a sister. You love her. Will you not let
her be your child? and I will be her sister in
heaven, and watch over you both. Shall it not be
so, mother? Alice has no mother, and you will
have no child. Will you not take her, mother, for
the sake of your lost Lily?" Then, joining their
hands, and looking at them fondly, "That is right,"
she said; "you will not love me the less for loving
Alice; and, when she plays upon my harp, you will
think of me and the golden harps of the angels."
Alice wept: she who had been so long motherless
realized all the fond blessing of such a love.

"I am not afraid to die," continued Lily. "God is my Father, and I know he calls me into his great love. Bring my friends now, and let me see them once more before I go home. Lily gazed earnestly at the little group gathered tearfully around her bed. For each one she had some token of affection, — a ring here, a book there, a ribbon or pressed flower to another. With saddened faces they received them, and the room was filled with their sobs. "Don't, dear friends," said Lily, "you distress me. When one returns from a journey and sees once more home faces, does he weep or rejoice? I am only going back to my Father's arms: you will see me there."

Lucy Howard wept passionately. "No, no, Lily! I shall never see you again. I shall not go to that 'better land.' You are an angel, I an evil spirit. God will reward you, and punish me. He cannot be 'my Father.' I am afraid of him."

"No, Lucy. God is love: he that feareth is not made perfect in love; for 'perfect love casteth out fear.' His love is above and around you, as a great light in darkness, — you cannot stumble or fall."

Lily lay back on her pillow exhausted; and one by one the girls left the room sadly and tearfully. "Heaven is full of angels," said Ellen Lee: "could they not have left us this one?"

Lily's eyes were closed. "Her life will pass with the hour," said the doctor.

Who that has watched a dear one passing down the shadowed valley, does not remember the hopeless feeling which filled the heart after the great struggle for resignation was passed; and the weary calm which came when Hope's ministers are fled; the whisper of " Peace! " when the human affection says " there is no peace "? — these are the heaviest crosses of affliction. Heavy indeed was the heart of Mrs. Cushing. She realized the fulfilment of her fear, that God would some time remove the idol she had dared to love better than him. Heavy indeed was the heart of the indulgent father, who watched the fading of his great hope.

The sun was setting. The curtains had been drawn, that Lily's eyes might look once more upon the purple heavens. A faint flush tinged her cheek, — who shall say it was not a reflection of the coming glory? Out in the west the sky glowed with warm, sun-kissed clouds; and all the light and sweetness and beauty seemed drawn from earth to illumine with celestial brightness the gates of eternity.

Who shall wonder if to the vision of departing faith heaven was opened, and the ridge of brightness seemed the rounds of a golden ladder, where ministering spirits ascended into glory? The dying girl lay as if in a glorious trance; and her spirit seemed passing on the strain of some heavenly melody. Once in a while she murmured, " Dear father! " when Mr. Cushing bent over her. The

sweet voice of Alice broke the stillness, — "'Let
not your heart be troubled: ye believe in God, believe also in me. In my Father's house are many
mansions. I go to prepare a place for you.'"
"More! more!" said Lily; "more of those beautiful words." "'And God shall wipe away all
tears; and there shall be no more pain, neither sorrow nor crying; for the former things are passed
away. Yea, though I walk through the valley
of the shadow of death, I will fear no evil, for
thou art with me.'"

"O mother! I can see it now, that beautiful country; it is light, — all light. There is no valley, and
no shadow. You used to call me your Lily-flower;
but the lilies grow larger and fairer there : some day
you will follow me into this bright land, where "—.
The pale lips faintly uttered, "Our Father;" the
light went out of the blue eyes, like the sunset flush
in the eye of day, and Lily was in heaven. Yes:
she had put her hand in that of the waiting angel,
and they had passed on together under the dark
portal of this life into the gates of immortality.

Alice remembered her words, — "I shall pass
directly in at the portal," — and turned her gaze to
the western sky. Amidst the fading crimson, one
little spot of blue was visible, — to her it was the
path made by the ascending spirits.

Mrs. Cushing sank upon her knees, and buried
her face in her hands. Her hope had faded, her

light had gone out, her heart was desolate. "'My God, my God! why hast thou forsaken me?'")urst from her in her agony. Urged by deep sympathy, Alice knelt beside her, and throwing her .rms around her neck murmured, "Mother." "My daughter," said Mrs. Cushing: "let us pray." And over the silent form went up the supplication of broken-hearted love, the prayer for strength and grace, till an inflow of divine love hallowed their grief, while it knit still closer the bonds of mutual affection. From that hour Alice felt she was not motherless.

In a beautiful spot at Greenwood they made the grave of Lily. The long branches of the willow swept over the stone which mourning love reared . above her dust, so that in summer the zephyr sang. a soothing symphony amid the leaves, and the soft sunlight cast around the stone a halo like a crown. It bore the simple inscription, "Our Lily," with a hand pointing upward, and the motto, *Resurrexi*, — "I have risen."

Years after this, when trial and sorrow had purified and enlarged her life, Alice stood by this stone, and, as she read the motto, so full of hope, with deep feeling repeated the sweet words of Ellen Lee: —

"Like a soft and tender vision,
Like a picture old and rare,
Seems this thought, this dream elysian,
Of a maiden young and fair.

'Tis a sad and simple story, —
    Where the sunset's gold was poured,
She ascended through the glory
    With the angel of the Lord.

So sometimes I dream at even, —
    If our lives are good and true,
We may one day go to heaven
    With the waiting angels too.

We may join the holy harping;
    We may lie upon His breast,
'Where the wicked cease from troubling,
    And the weary are at rest. "

CHAPTER XVI.

An unsensitive nature is seldom aroused, except it be on the occasion of strong passion or emotion. This was the case with Ada Whiting. Lily's sickness had affected her very little. She was sure she would get well, she said, — "there was no need of worrying." Sometimes her companions would reply, — "But suppose that Lily should die, would you not feel sorry for talking so?"

"Nonsense! Lily's health is as good as mine, usually. What is the use of fretting?"

And so Ada resigned herself to her own pleasures, heedless of the sacred obligations of friendly love. But it is well known, that, when these persons are surprised by an unhappy event, they are deeply afflicted. No one suffers so much as they; and they overlay the grief of others with their own lamentations. So it was with Ada: she was completely overwhelmed. She cried herself almost sick over the loss of her friend, and suddenly became aware of her lost companion's worth and many virtues.

In one of these moods Alice surprised her, as she was sitting in their room one morning. Her book was spread open on her lap; but her head was bowed upon it, and the tears trickled through her

6*

fingers.   She did not hear any one approach, and for
a few moments Alice stood regarding her in silence.

" What is the matter, Cousin Ada ? "

Ada raised her head, but quickly hid her face in
her hands again.

Alice stood a moment, her mind divided between
pity and vexation.   She, with her strong mind,
could have little sympathy with her cousin's fre-
quent crying spells, but she pitied her most sin-
cerely.   " I wonder what can be the matter now ! "
thought she.

" Are you sick, Ada ? "

" Yes, I am sick, — heart-sick," was the reply.

" What book have you there, cousin ? "

Ada condescended to wipe her eyes, and, taking
up the book, read off the title,—

" ' The Lone Heart ; a Tale of Love and Disappointment.'   And it's such a good book," she continued, " so affecting ; and it made me think so much
of my own troubles.   Nobody knows how many unhappy hours I have."

Just the slightest curve of contempt wreathed
Alice's firm lips.   She did not know whether she
ought to talk to her cousin, or leave her to cry over
her imaginary woes.   Seating herself, she said, —

" I consider it my duty to talk with you, Cousin
Ada."

" That everlasting word, — *duty*.   You talk to me
as if you were doing penance."

"No, Cousin Ada: you do me wrong. I *will* sympathize with you in any *real* trouble, and join you in any plan for our improvement. Any one can work himself into a morbid heartache who will read sentimental novels by the hour. Why, Ada, I have known girls who read novels so much they believed all sorts of foolish things. I have heard of one young girl who imagined she was not her parents' child, but that they stole her in infancy from her father, who was a great lord. And so she treated her poor father and mother as if they were her tyrants and enemies."

"I don't think that is so very wonderful," said Ada. "It wouldn't take much for me to imagine my father and mother were my enemies. I'm sure they never loved me any."

"O Ada! Ada! don't, pray don't. One of these days you will repent so bitterly saying these words. When your father and mother lie where mine do, you will wish every word you uttered had been a blessing. I'm sure, Ada, your mother is proud of you, and Uncle William loves you."

"Not half as much as he does you, Alice; and I'm sure you hit the nail on the head when you said mother was proud of me. She never loved me one bit. The first thing I can remember is being dressed up like a great doll, so that people might admire my black curls, and say, 'She is a little beauty, Mrs. Whiting, — looks just like her mother.'

I was brought up in that school. Is it any wonder that I am proud and selfish now?"

Alice said nothing, for she felt the truth of this; and Ada continued, — "I think sometimes, Alice, for all I am so vain and foolish, I love Miss Newton, I love you. I think it is better to be simple and loving; but I wouldn't change places. You will walk in the quiet paths of life. I must have stir, excitement; I want admiration. One day, Lizzie and I will have establishments of our own: then I will dance and dress! and, if there are any duties in life, I will forget them. You will pity me, and I shall pity you. Any thing is better than to be old-maidish, — a poke."

"May God bless you, my dear cousin!" said Alice solemnly; "and may no deeper disgrace ever attach itself to you than that of a single life! I am content to take life as God sends it. If it be marriage, with its trials and duties, I will not be so cowardly as to shrink back. If it be a single life, I know that there is work in the highways as well as in the vallies. I am not *afraid* to be an old maid."

Very sad at heart, Alice went back to her books. Ada watched her till the last flutter of her dress disappeared in the doorway, and then, burying her face in her hands again, thought more seriously than she was wont. The verbs in Alice's Latin Grammar lost their hard sameness, and instead she seemed to see sweet words of counsel and courage, and hear

voices long ago hushed. "O Father!" she murmured, "I thank thee that I had wise and good
parents."

And what thought Ada?

"My mother never loved me as Alice's mother
loved her, — never kissed me, never taught me
any prayers! O mother! perhaps I should not be
so selfish if you had loved me."

Ada Whiting had true cause for unhappiness,— a
cause which she did not reveal to her cousin. She
had pledged herself to do a deed unworthy of her,
and she already more than repented. Evelina Cobb
had never lost her influence over Ada, although her
shallowness and vanity had somewhat weakened it.
Ada liked her bold recklessness, her freedom from
all religious restraints, and her flattering words.
Evelina had never forgiven Charles and Ellen Lee
for the mortification they had caused her, and she
declared that she would be even with them. An
occasion was approaching which seemed to favor her
plans for revenge. The governor of the state was
personally interested in Miss Newton's school, and
he had promised a gold medal for the best essay at
the close of the coming term. There was much
rivalry in the school. Ellen Lee had always been
called the best writer; but now Ada had made every
effort to outdo her. Never did rivals at the Olym-
pian games strive with more eager zeal. Groups of
girls would assemble at recess to talk over the pros-

pects of the competitors. Ellen Lee's was a poetical essay, evincing great talent; and the pupils already looked upon her as the victor. This was very galling to Ada's pride.

All the worst traits of her passionate nature were aroused at the prospect of failure, and flowed out in bitter feelings towards her rival. If ever any one needed a true friend, Ada needed one now; but, alas! she fell into the hands of an enemy.

Evelina had read novels enough to know how to plot, and she could coax and flatter enough to obtain the instruments she needed. Her plan was this: She would obtain Ellen's essay the night before the exhibition, hide it where it would not come to light until after that occasion, and then seem like a pure accident, which no one could account for. Thus she would deprive Ellen of a triumph and a prize, while at the same time she would be revenging herself on both brother and sister. But it would never do for her to put this plot into execution herself.

Let us see how the monkey used the cat's paw to pull his chestnuts out of the fire. "You darling girl," said Evelina, as she met Ada at the foot of the stairs; "I've been dying to see you: come into the recitation-room, — I have fixed it splendidly," said she, as she drew Ada to a seat. "You see Miss Newton gave Bridget the key to the schoolroom this morning, in order that she might do the cleaning. Thinks I to myself, here's a chance: so after school

I just went down to the kitchen, and made a bargain with Bridget to let me have the key this evening. She was willing enough to do it for an old ribbon I gave her. Her brain is so dull she never will suspect me, even if questioned. Ellen's portfolio is in her desk, — I saw her put it there at the close of the session. So you see it is all arranged, and nicely too. Come, why don't you say what you think of it?" she continued, as Ada sat silent and moody.

"I believe I shall have nothing to do with it," said Ada: "it is too mean even for me."

"Give it up!" cried Evelina, "after I've had all this trouble for you? And so you're willing to slave a month over an essay, and then let the favorite take the prize! I wouldn't have taken so much trouble for you, if I had known you would give it up so meanly!"

"Who is the most accommodated, I wonder?" retorted Ada. "But the truth is, it does look beneath one to be creeping into the schoolroom at night, like a thief, — yes, a thief in reality. I believe I had rather lose the prize."

"Oh! well," said Evelina coolly, "you can go without it, I suppose. Nobody will cry if you don't get it. But how cheap Ada Whiting will feel!"

Ada's eyes flashed. The old jealousy was alive again. "Any thing is better than failure," thought she, — "I can bear any thing better than that. Besides," reasoned the tempter, "nobody will know it.

What is a moment's danger to the triumph of success?"

"I will do it," replied she. "What is the use of living if you can't have what you want?"

"And I may depend upon you?" said Evelina inquiringly.

"Yes: bring the key to your room at nine o'clock; and, when the house is still, I will go with you."

"You are a dear good girl," said Evelina purringly. "How mad Ellen Lee's friends will be! But they never will suspect in the world."

"Yes," said she, when Ada had left the room. "One good turn deserves another. That picture on the wall won't look so hateful after this."

CHAPTER XVII

As the bell rang for the girls to retire, Evelina entered her chamber with Ada. A half hour passed in conversation, during which time the noise in the house grew fainter and fainter, and finally ceased altogether. A hush, most of all impressive when it holds the thought of sleep, settled over them like a benediction, as they sat there silent and motionless. Ada was not naturally superstitious: but, with the sense of guilt on her mind, the silence seemed filled with mocking voices, and the darkness took strange shapes; while all the old goblin tales she had ever read seemed to haunt her imagination. Alas! she had not that pure heart which sees God, nor the pure lips to pray, " Deliver us from evil."

" Do you think every thing is perfectly safe?" ventured she, in a whisper.

" Yes," replied Evelina; "there is no danger if you are very careful. You had better take off your shoes when you go. We shall have good luck, for I saw the moon over my right shoulder to-night. What ails you?" said she, as she felt Ada shudder.

" Nothing," replied her companion. " Isn't it a little cold? I wish we had left the lamp burning. I feel a little faint."

"You will get over it in a minute," said Evelina.
"We mustn't light the lamp," for we should certainly be discovered.   I've got some lucifer matches
in my pocket, and you can light the gas when you
get down stairs.   Come," said she, pulling Ada's
hand, "I guess it's safe now."

But Ada drew it back.   "I wish you would go
yourself, Evelina.   I don't care for the prize so
much as to do this, — go yourself."

"Impossible," returned Evelina, putting the key
into her hand.   "I should be suspected immediately.
Come, you will feel better in a minute;" and she
pushed Ada before her into the entry.   The sleep-
ing-rooms were situated opposite each other, only
divided by a long entry or passage-way.   The doors
were mostly ajar; but there were no lights, nor any
signs of wakeful life.   They stole softly along the
passage, feeling their way by the wall, when suddenly Ada whispered, —

"What's that?"

The two girls stood holding their breath, while
from one of the rooms stole a softened murmur, a
prayerful voice, which Ada knew to be Alice's.
For worlds she could not have moved.   She felt like
the criminal compelled to hear his own death-war-
rant, while every word fell distinctly on her ear, -
"'And forgive us our trespasses, as we forgive those
who trespass against us.   And lead us not into
temptation, but deliver us from evil.'"

"Deliver us from evil, — deliver us from evil,"
— how the words echoed and re-echoed in her ears!
She said them over and over again with white lips
that made no sound; she clung to them as the
drowning man clutches at a straw, with a blind
sense of safety and hope in their spell. Then came
the dark thought, — "What right have I to take the
name of the Lord upon my lips? I, clothed in the
livery of sin, to be talking the language of heaven?"
They would do for Alice, and for the sinless lips of
little children ; but such words were mockery for her.
In an instant of time she seemed to live ages of
thought. "What would Alice think of this? what
would Lily think? Perhaps she was even then
looking at her. Perhaps God had sent her to be a
witness of her sin." The thought worked upon
her feverish, excited mind. She almost fancied she
caught a glimpse of white garments, and a super-
natural dread filled her with shrinking terror.

"Come, Ada," whispered Evelina, "it is nothing." But Ada stirred not a step, nor uttered a
word. "Come," said Evelina, shaking her, "what
is the matter with you?"

"Lead us not into temptation!" whispered Ada
softly. "Did you hear her say it? Lily said it!"

Evelina was frightened. She shook her companion rudely. "Are you crazy?" said she.

"Yes, I believe I am! — I wish I were!" said
Ada. "I wish we had a light!"

They moved on again softly, stopping now and then to listen. Oh! the still, calm, holy night — how eloquent its stillness! how fearful its calmness! how voiceful its holiness! How it searches out our weaknesses! — how its brooding darkness seems to separate us from the outward world, and leave us alone with God!

With cat-like tread they descended the stairs; the great clock in the hall seemed sounding an alarm, and its "Tick-tick-tick-tick" said in Ada's ears, "Thief-thief-thief-thief," till it almost mad-dened her. She stopped her ears, but only to hear another voice say, "Lead us not into temptation!"

"What a fool I am!" thought she. "I *will* go on now. What does that clock mean, I wonder? I'll beat it to pieces if it don't stop."

They reached the door of the school-room. Ada's hand was upon the knob, when, as she afterwards declared, a voice like a shout cried, "Lead us not into temptation." She turned and fled up the stairway with mad haste, and stopped not till she had thrown herself into her cousin's room, weeping and sobbing hysterically. It was a long time before she could answer Alice's eager questions.

"O Cousin Alice! you will despise me; but you can't hate me as I hate myself." And then she told the story of her temptation. "It was dreadful, Alice, sinful too; and, oh! so mean, — that cuts me worst of all! How can I ever hold my head up again?"

"Heaven be praised!" exclaimed Alice.

"Praised for what?—that I have lowered and degraded myself?"

"No!—that you were saved from the evil, Ada. What if you never could have held your head up in the presence of honor? I love you more this minute than I ever did before."

Ada sat thoughtful. "I wish I were like you, Alice. Do you remember what father said one night? 'Alice,' said he, 'will make the world better for her having lived in it.' I have thought of that so much!"

"Don't think of it any more then," responded Alice, throwing her arms affectionately around her cousin. "Measure your strength, not by the past, but by faith in the future. If your record-book bears the word 'unfaithful,' let the white leaves say, 'Well done! good and faithful servant.'"

"But then I am so impulsive, Alice, and all my impulses are wrong ones. You see I know what is right; but it is easier to do wrong. How can I help it? I wasn't made like you. If I had been made right, there would have been no trouble."

"That is not only sinful, but unphilosophical," replied Alice. "Because you have not developed your spiritual nature, you lay the lack of its gifts and graces at the door of Providence, while all around you are the means of culture. It is the blind eye only that looks downward upon Destiny and

Fate, while above there are the sunny hills of
Endeavor."

Ada sighed. "You have commenced climbing
those hills, Alice; but I am still in the valley
of Indolence. It is an enchanted place, and I
have no thread to guide me out of it. What shall
I do?"

"Open your eyes, Ada! Don't you see the
thread? There are two threads in your enchanted
valley, running in opposite directions. One is the
golden thread of Pleasure; and it shines so brightly
you can scarce see the sombre little thread of Duty.
The thread of Pleasure winds among the low valleys
of ease; and, if you follow it, it will lead you to the
dark river of Misery, and invite you to drown
Memory among the waves of Forgetfulness. The
other, the thread of Duty, winds along the dusty
highways of Labor, and wounds your feet by passing over the rocks of Temptation; but it leads you
up the Mountain of Aspiration, and shows you the
sunny slope of perfect Faith, whence you may catch
a glimpse of the glory beyond. Which will you
choose?"

Ada looked her admiration! The soul of Alice
seemed stirred with a hope new to her, — a hope
that her dear cousin would seek to find "that better
part" which should not be taken away from her.

"I ought to choose Duty," said Ada; "but I love
Pleasure better. To follow Duty, one must be re-

ligious, and religion makes people gloomy. I cannot give up the world yet!"

"I would not have you," returned Alice. "Only
make yourself worthy to help the world. It is no
heroism to run away from temptation."

"But you did not understand me, Cousin Alice.
I mean that I cannot give up the vanities of the
world. What shall I do when I go into society? I
want to make a sensation, — a triumph!"

"I did understand you too well, Cousin Ada. I
will tell you what to do. Take fast hold of the little
thread of Duty, and, as you mingle in these brilliant
scenes, show the butterflies of Fashion how a true soul
can live above their glitter. Carry the torch of Truth
among the dry chaff, and let it do its work. You have
a most glorious field for labor, — a true missionary
work, — if you would but do it. What will you say
when you give in an account of your stewardship?"

Alice's face glowed with impassioned fervor. It
was fairly radiant with *soul*.

"You are an angel, Alice," said Ada; "but between you and me there is a great gulf fixed. I
cannot see life as you see it. No one ever taught
me. My heart is heavy, and my brain is whirling.
Pity me, Alice, for I am very weak; and I cannot
think to-night. Do you believe I could be good,
Alice, if I should try?"

"Yes; but not by your own strength, Ada. Pray
that our Father will help you."

"I don't know how, Alice. I never said a prayer in my life."

"My poor cousin!"

"It is strictly true," said Ada. "I never remember hearing one in our house. I don't believe a prayer is said there from one year's end to another."

"If that is true now," said Alice, "don't let it be hereafter. Promise me that you will think of these things, Ada."

"I will see, Alice,—yes, I think I will try. For all you have no such splendid prospects in life, you are richer and happier."

Alice thought she would not have exchanged *her* "splendid prospects" for those of any queen or princess.

Ada's sleep was broken and uneasy that night; and more than once Alice was awakened by hearing her say, "I will try,—yes, I think I will try."

For herself, she rejoiced that this event had revealed Evelina in her true colors; and she hoped that now she might win her cousin to the society of truer friends.

The next morning revealed all. Evelina, rather than be cheated of her revenge, took the essay herself. Of course she denied all knowledge of it, not dreaming that Ada would say any thing of a matter which would criminate herself. But she, with her late remorse weighing heavily upon her mind, sought a private interview with Miss Newton, and told her all. She wept over her ungenerous conduct, and told Miss Newton of Alice's good counsels. Miss Newton herself wept at the recital.

"You cannot do better," said she, "than to regard this advice. A character like her's is beyond all price. As for Evelina, I think her influence is an evil one. I cannot have her longer under my care."

"Isn't it scandalous, girls?" said Jane Swift. "Who would have thought it of Ada Whiting? But it all comes of that prying Alice Morton."

Edward Hall heard the recital from the admiring lips of one of Alice's school-friends, who could not say enough in praise of her.

"This Miss Morton," said he, "is a noble girl. I believe I must know her better."

"Yes," said the judge, "I wish you would."

CHAPTER XVIII.

" WELL, little Miss Sobriety!" said Mr. Whiting, " does it seem good to be at home again?"

" Yes indeed, uncle!" and Alice's eyes seconded the answer. " But why do you call me little?"

" Oh! because I want you to be just as you were when I used to hold you on my knee and kiss you, as I am going to do now,"—and he imprinted a hearty kiss upon her forehead.

" Why, William, how can you?" said Mrs. Whiting. " Think of my poor nerves! Ada, *will* you stop drumming that piano? Goodness! it is a wonder how I ever live through so much."

It was Christmas Eve, and the family were all assembled once more in the drawing-room. The coal in the grate glowed as cheerfully, and the crimson curtains threw their shadows as warmly, as when we first saw Alice, on that rainy November evening, when Mr. Whiting granted her wishes. Fred sat very quietly on the sofa, which Alice thought was strange for him; and she wondered if the discipline of hard study had in any way curbed his mischievous impulses.

" Well, Frederick," said his father, " what are

you thinking of? You have done well to keep your peace for five minutes."

"Oh! I can be peaceable when I choose," said Fred, laughing; "but just now my thoughts were occupied by a very interesting subject."

"What, pray, did you ever think of for five minutes at a time?" said Lizzie.

"Most gracious sister," said Fred, "did time permit, I would enter into an abstruse and metaphysical analysis of my reasoning faculties, to convince you that I am capable of such an effort. To speak plainly, I am thinking of Alice. Don't you think she has grown handsome?"

Alice blushed.

"If I had a spy-glass, perhaps I could see it," replied Lizzie, tossing her head; "but I must say, No."

"Come, Lizzie, can't you be generous for once?" said Mr. Whiting. "For my part, I think Alice's bright cheeks would shame the lily faces of our city girls. I think the country air has made her quite beautiful."

"And so do I," said Fred.

"And I," said Ada.

If Alice's cheeks were bright before, they were now like a damask rose.

"How ridiculous!" said Lizzie; and the mother echoed, "How ridiculous!"

"You'll have to be careful, Lizzie," said her

brother wickedly, exchanging a glance with Ada, "or Alice will steal all your admirers. Come now, cousin, own up! How many hearts have you conquered with those brown eyes?"

"I have not yet conquered my own, Cousin Fred.

"But some one has conquered it for you, I suppose, and so saved you the trouble. Really, Cousin Alice, I am proud of you. Did you ever see a magnet, Lizzie? What if Louis ——"

"Stop, Frederick Whiting! Can you?"

"Perhaps I might, my angelic sister, if you were to request me politely," replied the provoking brother.

"Dear cousin," said Alice, pleadingly laying her hand upon his arm, "wont you stop for *my* sake? You make me very unhappy," — and her tearful eyes witnessed to her truth.

"My divine little Queen of Hearts, command me; for my own heart went long ago," — and Fred made a low obeisance.

"It seems that you have mastered the verb 'to love' since you have been at college," said Lizzie scornfully.

"And so have you," said Fred. "Be careful, Lizzie, of foreign noblemen."

Lizzie opened her great eyes half in surprise and half in anger.

"You don't know any thing about my friends."

" Don't I ? " said Fred, with a roguish twinkle of his eye. " Most adorable angel," said he, dropping on one knee, and imitating the exact tone of Louis Melville, " let-ah the light-ah of your beautiful eyes rest-ah upon me. My life-ah is in your divine-ah presence."

Lizzie's eyes flashed angrily.

" Did you hear that ? And so you were eavesdropping, were you ? Learned that at college, I suppose ? " ·

The scene was comic, and a smile passed through the group.

" Come, come, children," said Mr. Whiting, " do your lovemaking as you please, but let us be pleasant to-night. Wife, shall we have some music ? "

" I don't care, I am sure," said Mrs. Whiting. " One might as well be bored in one way as another. Lizzie, play your father that new Italian air."

" No, no; give me something that has soul in it. Ada, will you play ' Sweet Home,' and let Alice sing the words ? "

Alice sang it with expression. Her voice, soft and sweet, seemed more tender, as if Memory had melted her tears into the strain.

" That's very sweet," said Fred.

" Humdrum," said Lizzie.

The tears rained over Alice's face : she could not help it. The beloved tune had been an " open sesame " for many buried delights. It seemed so out of place, with its sweet lowliness, among those proud spirits and gilded trappings.

"Where is home, Alice?" said Mr. Whiting, as he stood leaning over her chair.

"Where the heart is, Uncle William. Mine is in heaven."

"I wish mine was," said Mr. Whiting, half unconsciously.

"For my part, I am very well contented to live here," said Lizzie.

"But you may not always be able to, my daughter."

"Why, what do you mean, father? You are not going to leave this house?"

"No, not at present," said Mr. Whiting, smiling. "I referred to the uncertainty of life."

"Oh! how you frightened me!" said Lizzie. "I was afraid something had happened. Henrietta West's father failed last week, and she's got to teach. If any such thing should happen to us; I should die. I never could live through such disgrace."

"Yes you would," said Fred. "Our wealth would be gone, but our trials and vexations of all kinds would be left."

Mr. Whiting looked troubled. "How little they dream," thought he, "that this splendor may be the sunset's last glory."

Alice remembered her old friends, John and Con-

tent.   She opened the kitchen-door softly: Content
was at the ironing table, her dusky face shining with
perspiration and good temper.   She did not perceive
that any one had entered; and Alice stole softly up
behind her, and threw over her head a gay bandanna
handkerchief.

"Lor' bress us! who dat?" and Content pulled
the trifle from her head, and stood peering curiously
at Alice, as if half inclined to think her an illusion.
But her eyes rested delightedly upon the handkerchief, and Alice feared that its bright red stripes
would outshine the giver.

"It's me, 'Tenty.   Don't you remember Alice?

"Bress ye, honey, yes!   Only ye looked so shinin'
like, and I'se been hopin' for ye so long.   I'se 'fraid
ye'd just melt away.   De dear chile! how handsome like she's growed," she continued, surveying
Alice with intense satisfaction.

"Then you're glad to see me, are you, 'Tenty?"

"'Pears like I'se joyful.   This 'ere 'kerchief is de
beautifullest!   'Clare for't, joyful as Jacob when he
seed Joseph, as ye used to tell for."

"Do you read the Bible now, 'Tenty?"

"Not much 'count, honey.   Ole John, he done
read some; but he circumwents it so dis chile don't
know nothin' 'bout it."

"I am glad you read it, at any rate," said Alice.
"Now I'm at home I will read for you."

"Thank ye.   I tell Old John, — ' Alice she's an

angel going straight to glory; but Missee Lizzie say she would not read for poor folks like me."

"Never mind, 'Tenty; if you are poor in this world's goods, I hope you are rich in grace."

" So I tole 'em," said Content, triumphantly.

Alice spent some time with her humble friends. When John came home, she took his well-worn Bible, and read sweet comforting passages, while the tears ran down the faces of her auditors. There is a spell in a low, musical voice; and some people have a faculty of melting their souls into their tones. Alice read chapter after chapter, feeling it a privilege to read the words of eternal life to the poor and unlearned.

" Now, John," said Alice, " I want to hear you read, so I can see how much you have improved."

" Dis child has made slow progress," said John, as he read, — "God so loved the world that he gave his only begotten Son, that whosoever believeth on Him should not perish, but have eternal life."

" Those are precious promises," said Alice, " and you read very well; and while I am at home I will teach you every day."

"Thank ye, child. 'Pears like I would have ye stay always with us, Miss Alice."

Very different from this was the scene in one of the upper rooms of this house of luxury.

" Ada," said Lizzie, as she stood before the glass, "I want you to advise me. You see we are all going to Mrs. Hammersford's to-morrow night, and all the world will be there. Now, what shall I wear? —

what color do you think suits my style of beauty
best? Now, there's red," she rattled on, "but that's
too flashy! and blue, — gentlemen can't bear blue!
and purple, or violet. There, I've got it now,
— violet would be just the thing; don't you think
so, Ada?"

"Really, sister, I don't know; suit yourself.
The color of a dress don't matter much!"

"What an innocent, unsophisticated thing you
are! Don't matter, do you think? I tell you the
color of a dress *is* every thing; you'll find it out
when you go into society."

"Then I am to suppose that society is made up
of dresses, varying in kind and quality according to
the market valuation of the person in them," said
Ada, half in earnest and half in raillery.

"Nonsense, Ada! What is the matter with you?
You've come home as moping and solemn and old-
maidish as you can be!"

"I believe I have begun to think a little, Lizzie."

"Begun to fiddle-stick!" exclaimed her sister.
"I tell you, you must not think! It'll just spoil
you for society. But I see that preaching Alice
Morton has been filling your head with her pious
notions. I told mother how it would·be! There is
nothing like a French Boarding School to fit one for
society!" Lizzie talked on, telling Ada of the
grand balls of the season, and enlarging upon her
own success, until Ada caught a part of her enthu-

7*

siasm.   Alice's simple . pleasure seemed nothing compared to the gay life of fashion; and, for the time, dress, company, and admiration, seemed the highest objects of earthly ambition.

" Never fear for me, Lizzie ; I always said I would make a sensation! Sometimes, when I talk with Alice, I feel as if the world was all vanity and show ; but I *know* I cannot live without admiration. Do you think I am handsome, Lizzie ? "

It was a tender point with Lizzie, but then this was an emergency, and she answered, " Yes, — very ! There is not one in a hundred who would make more sensation."

" Alice never told me I was handsome, in her life," thought Ada.

" You'll see something of society to-morrow night," continued Lizzie. " Look here, Ada, I am going to give you this set of pearls when you make your debut. They'll just suit your style."

Ada gazed, with glistening eyes, upon the beautiful ornaments. Her heart beat fast with hope and ambition. In their clear whiteness the future seemed painted. The festive scenes which should witness her triumph seemed to look out upon her, reflected from their silvery glow. The love and counsels of Alice were forgotten. Visions of beauty, of music, of bewildering revelry, came and went before her eyes, like fairy dreamings.

Alas, Ada! you thought you would "try."

So falleth human weakness, without the Divine Helper.

It was the happy Christmas Eve. Across the way, Mr. Whiting could see the windows of his neighbor's mansion brilliantly illuminated, and every now and then between the half-closed curtains he caught glimpses of merry, bounding children, and happy faces grew brighter still in the genial glow.

The drawing-room was deserted; there were no merry games there, no evergreen boughs, no candles burned in honor of the Christ Child. Only a lonely man sat and gazed into the dying fire, painting his own hopes and fears in its embers. He had to think of manhood passed, and opportunity wasted; of his soul's love and faith coined into gold, when it should have been poured out in heart-sunshine. Others, looking in that fire that night, might have seen the loving face of the risen Christ, and have heard the words, "Come unto me, all ye that labor and are heavy laden, and I will give you rest."

What did Mr. Whiting see? Alas! no shade so dark as that which comes between us and heaven! He saw no visions, he dreamed no dreams. His heaven was Wall Street; his angel faces, the hard features of unrelenting creditors; the great concern of his life, how to meet his payments.

But then, you know, reader, business-men have no time to think of such pretty poetical things! A dollar gained makes some show; but a step towards heaven, — why that's all theory.

A soft hand fell on Mr. Whiting's shoulder. He half shook it off; thinking, in his revery, that it was his creditor, Hardgrasp.

"Dear Uncle William, I wanted to say, 'Good-night.'"

"Good-night, dear, good-night!" But Alice thought he was strangely absent-minded; for, in-stead of dismissing her, he drew her gently to his side, and said, "You have come back the same, Alice. I am glad of that!"

"I was hoping a little better, Uncle William."

"How could you grow better, — any one so wicked as you are?" said her uncle, in mock seriousness.

"That is true," said Alice thoughtfully. "I have been thinking to-night how grieved dear mother must be to think I have come so far short of her last prayer for me."

"What was that, dear?"

"That I might be kept pure and unspotted from the world."

Alice's eyes were fixed upon her uncle. Neither spoke. The thought was a great one. Mr. Whit-ing's head sank low upon his breast, as if in com-munion with himself; and, when he again spoke, his voice was low and tender.

"I had a mother once, Alice, and she prayed

that prayer for me. One day she blessed me, and died. I was a wild, wayward boy then. I am a weak, wayward man now. Her prayer has never been answered. There, go now," he continued; " leave me alone awhile. I want to think."

Alice withdrew to her chamber. She was much astonished at her uncle's conversation. He never talked with any other member of the family as he did with her, — rarely ever with her, but when he did she saw how the crust of worldliness had hidden the true heart beneath. He had lacked an object for his rich affections. A long time Alice sat and mused; wondering if her Aunt Emily had ever really loved him, wondering if his dead mother had not been good and gentle like her own.

"ADA," said Mr. Whiting, as they sat at breakfast the next morning, "how much longer is your school-course?"

"About a year more, father. Why?"

"I am thinking that by next Christmas you will finish your studies. What do you intend to do then?"

Ada looked up in surprise. "Why, what should I do, father? I suppose I shall go into society, and make a use of my accomplishments."

Mr. Whiting took another muffin, and slowly buttered it, first on one side and then on the other. Finally he said, "Use, my child? Society itself is of no use. It holds enough empty idlers already."

"Really, father," said Lizzie, "you are complimentary to the rest of us."

"I am truthful, child. But what do *you* intend to do, Alice?"

"I shall teach, if possible," said Alice; "that has been my aim."

"You mustn't expect me to own you, then," said Lizzie. "I never *could* endure those prim schoolmistresses, sitting bolt upright by those everlasting green desks."

" I think it would require more condescension for Alice to own you," said Fred.

" Frederick," said Mrs. Whiting, with some show of dignity, " you may keep your opinion till it is called for."

" And what are *you* going to do, Lizzie ? " said her father.

" I ? Oh! I am going to Mrs. Hammersford's to-night. 'Have a good time now, and let the future take care of itself,' is my motto."

Her father smiled. " I am afraid the world never will reckon you as one of its benefactors, Lizzie."

" No, it never will, I am sure," she answered. " I am under no obligations to the world ; but it owes me a good time, and I am going to have it. The bee gathers honey from every flower, and so will I."

" A drone bee," said Fred. " Do you know what becomes of them, Lizzie ? "

" But what are you going to do, brother ? " said Ada. " Remember the old adage, — ' People that live in glass houses shouldn't throw stones.' "

" Oh! I am living on the strength of the good I am going to do by-and-by."

" And what may that be ? " His father also looked up inquiringly, fearing that something might have changed his aims.

" Oh! Alice and I have talked the matter over ; and we've come to the conclusion that the world is

all going wrong, and that it is necessary for me to study
law in order to put it to rights again.   Now, shall I
be a drone among all those herebys and aforesaids ?
Not much honey in law-flowers, — hey, Lizzie ? "

Mr. Whiting took his hat from the hall.   " I am
glad," said he, " that you have not chosen the mer-
cantile life ; for it is full of cares.   See, it does not
leave me even time for Christmas ! "

" Well, Lizzie," said her mother, " do you know
who are going to be at Mrs. Hammersford's to-
night ? "

" Oh ! all the *beau monde*, mother ; and I hear that
she has a nephew who will be there, — a young Mr.
Hall, lately from Europe.   They say he is perfectly
comme il faut."

Alice looked at Ada to see if she had noticed the
name, but she seemed pre-occupied.   " It could not
be the Mr. Hall we know," thought she.

Alice rose up with her ever-quiet soberness, and,
seeking her pretty chamber, resigned herself to one
of those long, silent self-communings, in which the
soul makes a pause and is silent ; while memory
hallows anew the past, folding again its white wings
over the relics of old buried joys and hopes and by-
gone sorrows.   In every deep, earnest heart there is
always a chamber whose door is locked and guarded,
and on the lock is written, " Holy."   But once in a
while, when some little chord of that heart is stirred,
— it may be only by some word or look or tear, or

when an anniversary recalls happy hours, — we will enter the sacred place alone, and with thought and prayer and tears consecrate it anew to the remembrance of our loves.

So it was with Alice. Christmas passed with her in resolutions for greater guard over herself, and in dreamings of olden happiness. Once more she lived over the happy Christmas days of her childhood. She saw the great chimney-corner, where so often a tiny stocking had hung; she remembered with what trembling eagerness she had drawn up the mysterious gifts, and heard the voice of her good father say, "May God bless my daughter!" Ah! "the sorrow of all sorrows is remembering happier things." It was a holy time with her when passion was banished, and the voice of the world was dumb. The tears trickled between her fingers, as one sometimes hears in the lull of the tempest the sound of the fast-dropping rain.

A knock at the door brought her back to the present. Chiding her weakness, she rose to answer the summons. It was Ada.

"Cousin Alice, Lizzie wants you to arrange her hair. She says you have so much taste."

It was an unwelcome task, for Lizzie was very fastidious. Alice's hands trembled some as she adjusted the heavy braids.

"Well, Ada, how does it look?" said Lizzie, when she had finished.

"Superbly: what fine taste Alice has!"

"Yes ; but then some can do these things better than any thing else," said Lizzie. "There, Alice, that will do. Now, Ada, help me clasp this bracelet."

Not even a "thank you" for poor Alice. In the hall she met Fred. His fine face was agitated by passion; and his usually easy, careless expression had given place to one of alarm.

"What is the matter, Cousin Fred? Aren't you going to Mrs. Hammersford's?"

"No, Cousin Alice: come into the parlor, I want to talk with you." He drew her to a seat, and, without answering her eager questions, commenced talking rapidly.

"You see, I went down to Mr. Cady's office to meet William, and, not finding any one there, I stepped into the back room, and took up a book. I know not how long I had sat there, till I heard father's name mentioned in an earnest conversation. I listened, and found that the two clerks were talking about the failures of the last week."

"'There's Sterne and Bros.,' said one, 'they're completely smashed up; and Arlington has "gone by the board," and so has Longstreet.'

"'Yes,' said the other ; 'and do you know that this last was largely indebted to Whiting? They say he owed him twenty thousand dollars, taking it all in all.' 'Yes, I heard of it this morning,' resumed the first. 'They say he found it as much as he could do to meet his last payments ; and, now the first of January is at hand, he will probably go by the board too. People thought he was safe as gospel, but I reckon he's on his last legs now.' 'Sure enough,' said the other confidently : 'extravagance and expensive habits have killed him. Why they say his daughters throw away money like water, and that fast son of his is enough to ruin a prince.' "

Fred was becoming very excited. His eyes were glowing with suppressed feeling, his hands were clenched, and he seemed altogether more like one beside himself than the easy, thoughtless boy he was.

"Dear cousin," said Alice, laying her hand on his arm, "don't tell me, if it makes you feel so badly. Wait till another time ! "

He shook her off almost rudely. "Yes, I will tell of it," exclaimed he ; " for it makes me mad ! A pretty piece of gossip they made of it to be sure ! — going on about our private business ; and wondering even whether the horses would be sold, and if old Greenleaf would buy them ; and what the house would probably bring if it were put up at auction."

" Cousin Fred ! "

" Yes ; and, to cap the climax, venturing some pretty little opinions of their own about pride, folly, &c. Now, Alice, what do you think of it ? " and Fred turned his glowing, excited face towards his cousin.

If he had attempted to read that face, he would
have found it a study. The sweet seriousness usual
to her still sat upon the high brow; the lines around
the mouth had lost their wonted firmness, and now
quivered with emotion, through which one might
still see an effort at stern self-control; and the lights
and shadows played alternately over her features,
expressing the hope and fear of the mind, — pity for
Fred, mingled with apprehension of coming evil.
One sometimes lives an hour of thought in a single
minute. So Alice saw her dream-castles vanish, and
her hopes and aims swallowed up in a threatening
cloud of evil. But the selfish fear was not enter-
tained, and she turned to answer Fred's question.
"I think," she said, "that my Cousin Fred has
heard a gossipping rumor, and is distressing himself
unnecessarily."

"But, Alice, you can't realize it, — you can't see
it as I do. To hear those sixpenny fellows using
our name like common property! It would have
roused even your cool blood."

"Have you any reason to think that Uncle William is involved?"

"I had not thought of it before this. But now I
remember that father has looked pale and careworn
lately. And, when I asked him for money yesterday, he put me off, and said something about difficulty in meeting payments. O Alice! if this
thing should come upon us, what will we do?"

" It is so sudden," said Alice. " I trust it is a mere rumor ; but at all events we must hope in God, and take courage."

" That's what you always say," returned Fred. " It seems to me, Alice, that your religion is a general panacea for all the ills of life. But it can't make the money we need, nor can it prevent an attachment by our creditors, — it don't do us any practical good ! And it makes you so cool about every thing. While I am in a fever of excitement, you sit and look at me like a Greek statue, as if we were not standing on the brink of ruin, as if we were not in danger of losing every thing worth living for."

" But I am not in such danger, Cousin Fred. Is the horizon of life bounded by the rim of a gold coin ? Heaven forbid ! "

" But what will you do ? Despicable as gold seems to you, it is the only source of comfort in this life. Honor, position, peace, circle in its circumference. What shall we do without it ? "

" Have we not mutual love, strong hands, willing hearts, my dear cousin ? " said Alice.

" All theory," said Fred. " I never can understand you, when you come upon these things, Alice. It seems more like a poet's song than a possible truth. I tell you, Cousin Alice, poetry and sentiment, and fine theory, will do very well on a sofa in an elegant drawing-room ; but take it in a homely kitchen, with the hands to work it out, instead of the mouth to speak it, and its robes of fine gossamer give place to common homespun, and its rainbow dyes to the dust and smoke of prosaic work."

Alice smiled. It was a sad smile, yet through it Fred could see the hope and courage of her soul. "You must excuse me, Cousin Alice," said he; "but I am afraid your moonshine would all melt away in sweeping a room or peeling potatoes."

"I will not boast, Cousin Fred. I do not know how much courage I should have. I hope the trial will not come; but, if it does, God helping me, I will do my duty."

"Forgive me, Alice," said Fred impulsively, kissing her cheek. "You are too good to live. One of these days, I shall see you flying away like the angels in our picture of the shepherds."

The generous love in Fred's face chased away the dark trouble that had brooded over it, as a burst of sunshine sometimes hangs a bow on the darkest cloud.

"There now, Cousin Fred, you begin to look quite like yourself again."

He rose to go, and the flush faded from his handsome face.

"We will hope for the best," said Alice, as she left the room.

The carriage that bore Mrs. Whiting and her fashionable daughters to the scene of display had rolled away from the door before Alice sought rest and thought in the drawing-room. Only one gas-burner threw a feeble light through the apartment, and seemed to melt every object into an indiscriminate haze. She did not turn on the gas, for she liked the soft twilight-like shadow better. She could see the little marble clock on the mantel-piece pointing to the hour of nine. The coal in the grate burned low, and the pictures on the walls rested half in light and half in shadow. Alice nestled down in the window-seat, and drew the crimson curtains around her. Here, for the first time, she began to question with herself. Why was she left alone in that great house? Why had not Mrs. Hammersford invited her? To be sure, she was not acquainted with her ; but then neither was Ada. Then it occurred to her that probably Ada had been introduced through Lizzie ; and she knew that Lizzie never would speak to her fashionable friends of her plain, unbrilliant, home-like cousin. No: she did not wonder now. The thought cost her a moment's pang ; but Alice had known too many *real* sorrows, had seen too much of life, to be long disquieted because a vain, giddy girl had not seen fit to notice her. Her thoughts referred to Lizzie's breakfast-table conversation. This young Mr. Hall, — who could he be? "A nephew of Mrs. Hammersford, lately from Europe!" Could it be the same? No: he had never mentioned having any relatives in New York. Then her mind turned back upon itself, and tried to analyze its thought. Why should she care? Why should she think of Edward Hall at all? She tried to dismiss the subject; but as often it returned again, with this disagreeable reflection, — What if it should be the same? He would see Ada there, and inquire for her. What would he think of it?

Alice heard her uncle's step in the hall. Her first impulse was to fly and open the door for him; but, with a dull, heavy tread he passed on, and Alice heard the library door close after him. Here was a new cause for apprehension. Her uncle never went to the library in the evening, — he always sat in the drawing-room. Again: all his family knew that when he went there it was upon business, and that he never liked to be disturbed. She felt anxious and lonely. She longed to go to her uncle to pour out her affection, and to cheer him with little offices of love; but she would not intrude on his privacy. So she drew the crimsom curtains yet closer around her, and thought of the threatening evil which brooded over her uncle's affairs. She had never dreamed of her uncle ever failing, for he was reputed immensely wealthy. Then she thought of her hopes and plans,— of her studies almost completed, of the honorable place she hoped to hold as a teacher; and felt that she could not give them all up. She looked at her hands, — they were soft and white. Would they be able to earn a livelihood!

Would she be a burden or help to her uncle? Should she stay there, or go out into the world?´

So Alice thought on, imagining what she should do in case their fears were verified, yet hoping all the time that it would prove a mistaken rumor. The little clock slowly struck eleven, and its tones called back her wandering thoughts. "What can be the matter with Uncle William?" thought she. "Two whole hours in the library, and no supper! What if he should be sick!"

She went into the kitchen. Only one little taper glimmered on the table, yet giving light enough to discover Content fast asleep in a corner.

"Content! Content!"

"Yes, massa!"

"It's me, 'Tenty. I want you to get me a candle."

"Oh! it's Missee Alice. I've been dreaming of the New Jerusalem, bress de Lord! Ole 'Tent soon be in heaven."

"Well, well, Content, if you're awake, get me a candle. Where's Sam?"

"He done gone wid Ole John, honey. He not much 'count no ways, so I tole him to take hisself off."

"You must keep awake, Content; for the family are away, and I'm going into the library."

She stole to the library door on tiptoe, and stood a moment listening. There was no sound. She

8

rapped softly, and bent her head, expecting to hear her uncle's voice say, "Come in." Still there was no sound. Once, twice, three times she repeated her timid knock; but the door remained firmly closed, and the same mocking stillness was the only answer.

Alice was alarmed. In her eager love she saw her uncle sick, perhaps dying; and, turning the knob softly, she entered. By the soft rays of the study-lamp, she could see her uncle bending over a heap of closely written papers, wholly absorbed in his work. He did not even notice her entrance, but kept on rapidly sorting out old papers, and casting up accounts with an unwearied pen.

It was a most uncomfortable position. Alice did not know whether to retreat softly or speak to him. She put down her candle on a table, and stood watching him at his labor. His face, so mild and beautiful in repose, was now marked by heavy lines, as if of care or watching; his broad, white forehead was knit, as if in intense thought; and the lips were compressed as if in pain. The expression of the whole face was one of haggard anguish. Surely, one looking upon it for the first time might hope it was not an index to the mind.

The stillness of the room was only broken by the hurried movement of Mr. Whiting's pen. Alice hardly dared to breathe. She dreaded, and yet almost hoped, that her uncle would discover her.

Still he wrote on, and still she could not gather courage to address him. Suddenly the busy hand stopped its work, his face relaxed into a look of utter weariness, and he sank back in his chair with a deep groan.

Alice sprang forward, with utter self-forgetfulness. "Dear Uncle William, what is the matter?"

"Why, child, how came you here? This is no place for you."

"I know it," returned Alice; "but I was afraid you were sick. Will you forgive me?"

Alice had a peculiar faculty for never being refused any thing. Mr. Whiting had looked grave, but now his brow softened. "Where is your aunt and the girls?" asked he.

"Gone to Mrs. Hammersford's soirée; and Fred has not yet returned from his club."

"The butterflies of fashion," he muttered. "How will they bear the winter with their painted wings?"

"Dear uncle, you are weary and half sick. You have forgotten your supper. Come into the dining-room, — you will feel better then."

"No, Alice, I am not hungry. You had better go back to the drawing-room. I am very busy."

"But, uncle, I wish you would have some supper. I will pour out your tea myself. Don't you want me to?"

Mr. Whiting drew Alice towards him, and put her on his knee. His face was very, very grave.

A long time he looked into her eyes, till she dropped their lids beneath the searching gaze.

"Little Alice, do you love me?"

"So much! Uncle William!"

"But do you love me, or my wealth? Would you love me as well if I could give you none of the advantages you have now?"

"Dear uncle, what have I done that you should doubt me? Did I not love my father and mother? They were poor. Next to them, I love you best."

A tear stole down Mr. Whiting's face. Alice had not seen him weep since the day he stood beside her mother's death-bed.

"Thank God," he said, "I shall have one treasure left!"

Alice counted one more Sheaf in the Harvest of Love.

CHAPTER XX

THE morning papers were full of the "great failure." Edward Hall laid them aside, and thought of the dazzling beauty of Lizzie Whiting, the belle of 'yesternight. *Sic transit*, said he to himself. Then he remembered his promise to call that morning.

He ascended the long flight of marble steps, and was ushered into the drawing-room. While awaiting Lizzie, he looked over a number of daguerreo-types which lay upon a side-table. One by one he put them aside: they were the faces of strangers. But why did he pause, and gaze earnestly at one? Why did he start, as if in a sudden surprise? Surely he had seen that face before. It could be no other, —it was the face of Alice Morton!

"Miss Whiting," said he, when they had ex-hausted memories of last night's soirée, "will you tell me who this picture represents? It reminds me strongly of a friend I once knew."

"That? Oh! that's my cousin, Alice Morton. She has lived six or seven years with us. Her parents died when she was quite young, and mother took her out of sheer charity."

It was a wonder that Edward's look did not

freeze Lizzie. "I am well acquainted with her," said he; "and she is one of my most valued friends. I shall do myself the pleasure to call and see her. Good morning, Miss Whiting." And Edward bowed himself from the room.

From this time Lizzie had another cause for disliking Alice. She had wounded her vanity.

The failure of Mr. Whiting was complete. The fashionable world, which had smiled on their success, now turned to them the cold shoulder, and talked openly of their folly and extravagance. An attachment was put upon their house and property, and they must leave their present home in a month. If some creditors, more lenient than others, had not compassionated their distress, they would have been wholly stripped of their property. Adversity shows up the character. Mr. Whiting, nervous and sensitive, shut himself up in his room, away from the sight of his friends. Mrs. Whiting lay really sick with a low fever. She was irritable and nervous to the last degree.

Of course all hope of the girls' return to school was abandoned. The family took their meals almost in silence, and the great rooms below were shut up in dreary gloom. Two weeks had passed since Christmas, and as yet no plan had been decided upon in regard to their future. Mrs. Whiting would not have exerted herself to think of these things, even if her health had allowed ; and Ada and Lizzie seemed paralyzed by the shock. Fred was moody and desponding. There was no one to rally the sinking energies of the family.

Mr. Whiting made no effort. He looked back upon his life as upon a wasted heritage. " I wasted my substance in riotous living," he said, " and now it is given to another." He avoided the society even of Alice and his children, for he thought he saw reproach in their faces.

One day a letter was put into Alice's hand. The well-known handwriting of Ellen Lee met her eye. "Only think, dear Alice," she wrote, "I am to enter on my duties as teacher next week. Now no more buffetings with poverty, no more taunts. The sky is clear blue, and hope has painted a beautiful rainbow over it. By the way, I forgot to tell you that mother and I have decided to move, that we may live near the institute. It will be much pleasanter, you know, for me to live at home. So the old house will be shut up, unless some one will rent or buy it. Wouldn't you like to take it as a summer residence? I am laughing at my folly, Alice, in asking such a question. It would be funny, indeed, to see your uncle's fine family in our homely rooms. Brother Charles is doing finely : report says he bids fair to become a finished artist. Grandpa sends love. I am so proud and happy, Alice, I don't know one now that I envy."

Alice thought of Ellen's hopeful future. Her's

had been hopeful once, but the cup had been dashed from her lips when it seemed overflowing with happiness. She crushed the letter in her hand, and bowed her head upon it ; while her heart sent forth an earnest prayer for faith and strength. There was nothing left but prayer ; but this was enough for Alice. She remembered the promise, "Thou wilt keep him in perfect peace whose mind is stayed on thee." Slowly hope and courage came back to her. She had been fed with manna in the wilderness.

"Lord, evermore give me this bread," she said aloud. "Realize to me the promise, that in due time we shall reap, if we faint not."

"Alice !" said a voice near her. Mr. Whiting took a seat beside her. Alice thought he looked ten years older, so well had care and trouble told their story in his face.

"Alice," said he, "I have ruined your hopes too. No wonder you pray, — I wish I could. I have even more need, for I fear even my own little Alice may take away her love for me."

"Oh, Uncle William ! pray don't talk so ! I'm happy, — yes, very happy," she repeated to herself, as if striving to make herself think so even against the dull, weary beatings of her heart ; "we shall all be happy together. And you and Aunt Emily and we children will all love each other very much. See ! do I not look hopeful ? I feel really strong, and would like to go to work right away if I only knew what to do. Haven't you something that I can do for you?" she said, putting her cheek close up to her uncle's, and smiling, although, in spite of her effort, the smile was a sad one.

" Yes, dear," he answered fondly, "you can pray for me. Perhaps the prayers of two angels — one in heaven and one here — may prevail. You were talking about work. Do you think those little white hands would bear soiling at hard labor?"

"Oh, yes indeed, uncle! Only tell me what to do. Try me and see."

Mr. Whiting's face brightened somewhat. "Let us see," he said, — "what can you do? what qualifications have you? How would little Miss Sobriety look at a churn or over an ironing-table?"

" Very well, I think, uncle," said Alice demurely.

"Perhaps I shall put you to the test. How would you like to live in the country, and milk cows, and make your own bread and butter?"

Alice's eyes sparkled. Visions of free, green meadows and country air, and whole depths of blue sky, already rose up before her.

" Are you going? Oh, I hope you will, Uncle William! You know I am a country girl myself. How fine it would be! I should have a flower-plot, and a peony and honeysuckle over the windows; and we would have plenty of light and air and sunshine. When are you going, Uncle William!"

8*

"I didn't say I was going, did I?" said Mr. Whiting.

"Now, uncle, don't plague me," said Alice; for she saw her earnestness had amused him. "I am going to sit on your knee, as I used to do, and you shall tell me all about it. Come, uncle, tell me a story, — 'please,' as the children say."

Mr. Whiting stroked her brown hair, and drew his arm around her.

"Years ago," he began, "on the banks of the Hudson, there stood a pretty white cottage. It was a sweet, fairy-like spot. Even in all my many rovings, I can remember nothing half so beautiful; and my love returns to it as the faithful needle points to the polar star. That was my home. My father was an honest, open-hearted farmer, proud of his broad acres, of his wife and son. I have been said to resemble him much. I have his brown hair and blue eyes. No one that I have ever seen *could* resemble my mother. When all my father's sternness was required to check my fiery impulses, a word or look from her brought me submissive to her feet, as David's harp charmed the passionate Saul. In this peaceful solitude I grew from childhood to youth, from youth to manhood. My father, despite his quiet tastes, was ambitious, and hoped his son would take a place in the world higher than his own. I read the lives of distinguished men, of successful merchants; stories of the fame and glory of the old world; Homer and Virgil at school, — till my young heart glowed with their ambition, as many a youthful heart has and will again. My mother always shook her head at this course of reading. 'Youth is headstrong and foolish enough of itself,' she would say. 'I am afraid it is not the.best thing to develop a character.' 'Nonsense, Mary,' my father would say: 'the boy has spirit. I want to see him make his mark in the world. He must win his spurs, and I shall help him do it.'

"Years brought changes to us. From a wayward boy, I became a headstrong youth. Even my mother's prayers and tears could not keep me from my long, daring rambles; and often I would be absent from home a week. One soft June day (shall I ever forget it?) I came home through the woods, where I had been roving for three days. I entered the house in my usually boisterous manner, when one came to me with a hush upon his lips, and told me that my mother was dead. She had died, and left me her blessing; but I was like the prodigal, without his hope. I went into the room where my mother lay, and gazed upon her still, white face. If tears will wash away sin, I believe I wept enough to blot out a multitude. I had stood in my own strength. I believed that my mother belonged to me of right, that it was necessary and proper she should love me as she did; but, beyond this, I believed all love was a myth. The sight of that still

face took the pride out of me; and the love which
ever before I had considered a weakness pulled at
my heartstrings with a force which no philosophy
could withstand. Suddenly from one of the shut·
ters a little ray of sunlight stole in, and rested
upon the face of the sleeper. As if a blow had
struck me, I started back. My mother's words flashed
over me: ' My son,' said she, ' when I took the
vows for you at your baptism, a beautiful ray of
sunlight stole in and rested upon your face. And I
hailed it as an omen that you would be a sunray in
the world, — a blessing to me and others.' Alas!
was not that sunray a condemnation?

" I was never, from that time, quite what I was before. I was still proud and ambitious, and self-
reliant: but my heart was like a magazine when a
spark falls into it; for, if ever any one spoke the
name of my mother, or I saw a face which recalled
hers, my feelings would bear down pride in one
passionate outbreak as fierce as the first. To this
hour the sunlight has for me a faded glory ; and a
beam streaming through some crevice into a room
has power to move me as nothing else can."

Mr. Whiting spoke with difficulty, as if the words
choked him, and Alice felt a tear drop on her hand.
Her own fell fast. " I did not think, uncle," she
said, " that your story would be so sad."

" Other years passed on. My father died, leaving me his blessing, and a small fortune, with which

to begin life. I listened to the song of ambition, and my battle-field was the mart of trade. I learned to drive a sharp bargain, and to glory in overreaching a rival. I made myself a name and fortune, and married, as it was said, 'very advantageously.' But at last the world and my ambition have deserted me. Weary of life, disgusted with the world, my only prayer is that I may die in peace. My old home has passed into the hands of strangers; but I wish to seek some quiet country place where I can rest from the turmoil of life, and, if possible, grow open-hearted and generous once more."

Alice grasped her letter as if a sudden thought had occurred to her. If her uncle intended going into the country, he might like Elmwood Village, and perhaps he would buy the Lee Farm. And that would be so near the seminary. Who knew? — perhaps she might be a teacher even yet. With trembling diffidence, she placed the letter before him. He seemed favorably impressed, and asked her many questions relative to the place, inquiring about the house, land, society, &c.

"The farm is a beautiful and rich one," said Alice; "but the house is old. If it were repaired, however, I think it would be a very pleasant dwelling. Should you rent a house, or buy, uncle?"

"I shall probably buy," replied he. "I have personal property which my creditors cannot touch, sufficient for this. I will think of it. I like Elmwood very much. It is quiet and rural. I think possibly I may buy this place."

From this time, Alice felt as if the matter was the same as settled.

CHAPTER XXI.

"For life is but a struggle of base will
With intellectual purpose."

"A LADY in the parlor, to see Miss Alice."
Alice started up from the chair where she had been
sitting, in the midst of trunks and boxes, and commenced arranging her somewhat disordered dress.
It was but a week before they would leave the city,
and the house seemed in one constant tumult, save
when Alice undertook to draw some system out of
the chaos. Lizzie and Ada, unused to care or labor
of any kind, grew impatient over the most trivial
duties, and finally would throw them by in dis-
gust. Fred spent most of his time away; for he
could not bear, he said, to see their home so dese-
crated. In fact, this misfortune had had a painful
effect upon Fred. He was gloomy and obstinate;
rarely saying any thing at home, and then never a
pleasant word. He had a mercurial disposition, —
happy or sad, according to circumstances; and consequently his spirits were now below zero. All his
sharp raillery and sparkling fun degenerated into
bitter sarcasm, which he delighted to pour out upon
Lizzie, for the bare pleasure of witnessing her anger.
Edward Hall was his favorite topic. He had called

upon Alice, as he had promised; and Fred was not long in discerning his sister's discomfiture. Consequently, Lizzie heard all about the little boy who didn't eat his supper, because he couldn't get it, and sundry stories about rockets that came down sticks, and other consolatory suggestions. This usually ended in a fit of tears on the part of Lizzie, and a complaint to her mother, who ended the matter by saying that her children were her plagues, and her health miserable, and she didn't know what was going to become of them all.

"I wonder who it can be!" said Alice, as she descended the stairs.

The softened light which came through the heavy curtains revealed a lady dressed in black, seated upon a couch. Her face was shaded by a mourning veil; but Alice's heart gave a quick bound, and, springing forward, she grasped the stranger's hand with a warm pressure.

"My dear Mrs. Cushing!" she exclaimed, while her eyes spoke a double welcome.

"Call me mother, Alice; it was *her* wish, you know."

How that trembling voice recalled Lily's! In spite of herself, Alice's eyes moistened. The memory of their lost one seemed floating around them, sanctifying their hearts with a loving and holy influence.

"She was my only treasure, Alice," said Mrs.

Cushing; "and her loss seems as fresh to me to-day as it did then. Listen, Alice," she continued. "I have come here to make a proposition to you, in which my whole heart is interested. I have never forgotten my dear Lily's last wish. She loved you as a sister; and my heart yearns towards you as a child. The beautiful form of my child-angel comes to me in my dreams, and joins our hands together as she did then. O Alice! may I hope it may be as she wished? My heart is empty and desolate. Lonely and broken-hearted, I have come to give you that heart, if you will live in it and bless it; to pour out its affection upon my Lily's sister, and make her my own true and rightful child. Alice, can you let me go back to my desolate home, with nothing to love or live for?"

Alice leaned her head upon the couch, and wept unrestrainedly. The sweet, pleading tones had such a soft tenderness in them, mingled with great sadness, that Alice felt as if she would like to throw her arms about her friend's neck, and rest in this safe asylum. But she must think, before she gave herself away. Her uncle had given her a home, and educated her. As long as she could benefit them, did not her duty say "Stay!"

Mrs. Cushing had been watching the many changes which came over Alice's face. She had not anticipated any hesitancy on her part, for she knew she had never been entirely happy at her

uncle's.   But Alice thought of her uncle's words,
"Thank God, I shall have one treasure left!"   Her
conversations with him had shown her how dear she
was to him, — how much she had grown into his
love.   Could she leave him, even for a mother's love
and a princely inheritance?

"No, mother," she said, "it cannot be.   My uncle
looks upon me as a daughter.   There is no one in
Uncle William's family that has known poverty, or
who can comfort him in his affliction.   I believe I
may help them a little; perhaps show them the
higher good, which lies all around us, if our eyes
could but see it, and were not blinded by the glitter
of gold.   I feel how great is the sacrifice I shall
make, but it is a cross I must bear for duty; and I
know that the dry wood of many a cross has budded
and blossomed, and borne heavenly fruit."

She had risen in her emotion, and now stood with
clasped hands and tearful eyes looking into Mrs.
Cushing's face.   Surely, could that high thought
and noble speech be mere affectation?   Could that
be a theory which would melt away in the smoke of
a homely kitchen?   Such sublime trusts are never
found by logic.   They are the outbreathings of a
spirit at one with the Infinite Love.   They are the
expression of a patience and hope born of Christian
principle.

Tears fell over Mrs. Cushing's face.   "I ought
not to have expected so great a thing," said she.

"I suppose I am not worthy yet." She talked long with Alice, — reminded her of the labor and trial of poverty, and of the weariness of the hard world; but Alice replied in the same lofty language, though with tearful sadness.

She rose to go, and extended her hand in parting, — "God give you strength and grace, my dear one, that whatever path you tread may be brightened by the knowledge of a good life; and may our Father give his angels charge concerning you! One thing more, dear Alice, — will you come to me whenever your duty tells you you may?"

A weeping assent, a clasp of the hand, and she was gone. Alice sank down upon the couch, and, burying her face in her hands, tried to think. In the world of fashion this would have been called a grand chance. Few could have withstood such temptations as money, dress, ease, — to say nothing of the opportunity of polish and education. Alice believed not in enjoying for its mere sake, but in doing. She held that every desire, every ambition and love, should be crucified, which kept the soul from walking in the straight path of duty, or reaching its highest development. Such a doctrine annihilates selfishness. But there was another and yet stronger temptation. Mr. and Mrs. Cushing were going abroad. He had been chosen minister to a foreign court; and his wife was to go with him, that she might forget her recent sorrow in the midst of new

scenes.   What temptation could well be stronger to
a mind with an exquisite love of the beautiful in
nature, art, and humanity?   As the daughter of a
United States Minister, the very noblest society
would be open to her.   Was it not something to
be thought of?   Had she decided wisely?   All
these thoughts crowded upon her.   That night, in
the stillness of her room, she gave these doubts full
audience; weighing pleasure against duty, desire
against conviction, "the baser will against the intellectual purpose."   The fair halls of that beautiful
home rose up before her; the harmony of a life shel-
tered from the rude blasts of poverty and the world
might be hers.   The blessing of a mother's love and
the kind hand of a father were offered her, yet she
would not reach forth her hand and take them.

"There is yet time," whispered stubborn Desire.
"Your whole soul protests against such a sacrifice.
Go to Mrs. Cushing, and tell her so."

Then rose up a vision of gay Paris, and blue-eyed
Venice, and soft, dreamy Italy. - Her feet might
wander in the shades where Dante mused and Tasso
sung; she might pluck a leaf from the tomb of Virgil.   In that hour, she felt how strong her enthusiasm could be.

Then another thought came which had never
occurred to her before.   Perhaps she would be
accounted a burden in her uncle's family.   Could
she bear this?

Oh strangely mysterious human heart! Like the strings of a harp jarred by some rude hand, so human passions drown its sweet harmonies in harsh and stirring discords. So is it with us all, till the breath of prayer wakens the golden strings, and the hand of the great Harper, passing over them, fills the life with the harmonies of love and faith.

Months after this, in her distant country home, Alice heard that Mr. and Mrs. Cushing had sailed for Europe. If the thought cost her any pang, it was known only to her own heart; for she had never said a word concerning it to her uncle. With her usual energy and self-forgetfulness, she entered upon her work, — now here, now there, and everywhere with words of counsel and courage to the weaker spirits around her.

Mr. Whiting's creditors, more lenient than usual, allowed the family many household articles to which they had become endeared. Lizzie's piano went with them, and the choicest of the pictures, with the family portraits. The library was sold; but many good and valuable books were retained, as the property of Fred and Alice. The expense of servants was out of the question. So John and Netta were dismissed; but Content, being an old and valued servant, was retained to aid them in their new home. And Mr. Whiting also deemed it expedient to engage the services of our old friend, Samuel Lockling ; since, having been bred on a farm, he would make a very good farm-boy.

So, when the spring opened, the family left the city and their fashionable friends, and went, as Mrs. Whiting said, to " live in the back-woods." The village of Elmwood welcomed them with springing flowers and budding trees ; and the fresh breeze kissed their cheeks, as Alice said, " in pity for their weary-heartedness." The old house had been well fitted up, and a neat piazza added in front. Fred and Alice arrived a day or two before the rest; while Mr. Whiting went back for his wife and daughters. Alice was delighted with every thing ; and her light spirits raised Fred's to such a degree that he complimented the house for its very age and picturesqueness, and said the arrangement of the furniture was very tasteful.

" Yes ; and, Cousin Fred, don't you think these pretty Venetian blinds are better than the stiff shades they have in the city ? " said Alice.   " And I have had honeysuckle planted to run over the piazza ; and altogether I believe its going to be charming. I shall enjoy it !   Shant you, Fred ? "

" I don't know, Alice.   I suppose I shall in time ; but at present I think its rather dubious enjoyment. There's no club, and no lyceum, and no society worth looking at." .

" Why, there's Judge Hall, and his family. They are very kind, and polished too. And then, cousin,

you must forgive me, but I think I'm really glad
that there is no club here. It took so much of your
time. You will talk to me now more, and we can
read together in the long winter evenings. Wont
that be better than the club. Say, Fred, shan't you
like it better ? "

. Fred answered the question with a half pleased,
half puzzled look. " Yes, Alice, I suppose I shall in
time. I don't mean any thing uncomplimentary ; but
then women can't understand these things, — tisn't
to be expected they will, you know."

" Certainly not," said Alice, with her quiet smile,
which vexed Fred more than a hundred words
would have done. " I would not dare to meddle
with the weighty matters of the law."

" She does understand me too well," thought
Fred, " and thinks I am a useless, selfish article,
labelled, ' Frederic Whiting,' fit only for holiday-
dress and fair weather."

" Come, cousin, I'm going to be your doctor out
here, and I think a long face an unfavorable symp-
tom. Come, I've got something to show you." And
she fairly spirited him away through the great
kitchen into the sitting-room, and finally stopped to
take breath in a little room on the west side of the
house, which looked as if it might have seen service
as a store-room. But, whatever might have been its
unromantic service in times past, it was evident that
busy hands had been at work there, relieving its

plainness by little arts of grace and refinement. The apartment scarcely exceeded the limits of a common sleeping-room; but a neat carpet covered the floor, a pretty centre-table stood in the middle, of the room, and statues and vases looked out from every corner like reminders of "auld lang syne." Fred's eyes lighted with a genuine pleasure. "Why, Alice, this is delightful! Who fitted it up? and what is it for?"

"It's our studio, Fred. I remembered the room. The Lees used it as a clothes-room: but I teased Uncle William to have it fitted up; and I was here all day yesterday, finishing it, and now it only lacks the books."

"Dear Alice!" broke in Fred.

"No, I'm not dear at all! Every thing is cheap in the country. And look here," she continued, throwing up the sash, "here is a whole bed of English violets; and the west window too. Wont it be delightful at sunset?"

"Every thing is delightful where you are, Alice. You make me ashamed of myself. While I sit with idle hands, railing at Fortune for her ugly freak, you go to work and *do* something to make yourself and other people happy. And yet I think you feel misfortune as much as I do. I wish I had your secret."

The gay expression of her face sobered in a moment. Laying her hand upon his arm, she said softly, " You will not find it in your club or lyceum, Cousin Fred; but it lies deeper down. ' Trust in the Lord, and do good.' I try to take that as my rule. But, Fred,"— and the old brightness came back to lip and brow, —" I am waiting for you to help me unpack the books. I shall have to help Content with the supper soon."

" You are not going to do any such thing, Alice. I don't believe there is any need of coming quite so low as that."

" Oh, I love to ! " said Alice, The little library looked as cozy as could be, when they had finished, and justified Alice's words of satisfaction.

" Just enough books to go round, Fred ; " and then she left him there, till the bell rang for tea.

CHAPTER XXII

THE OLD HOMESTEAD.

THE gray twilight that streamed into Alice's window the next morning brought to her mind the thought that that day must be a busy one for her, since the rest of the family would be there by noon. Many arrangements still waited to be worked out by her busy little fingers; and, long before Fred and Content were stirring, Alice had made a pilgrimage through the rooms, to see that every thing looked as well as it possibly could, and to put a finishing touch here and there.

She passed through the great kitchen, over the yellow-painted floor, and, safely sliding the bolt of the back-door, stood in the open air. Those who have lived in the country know that a breath of country morning air is a very different thing from the scarce cooled atmosphere of the city. For a moment Alice felt nothing but thankfulness that she was once more under the broad arching skies, and permitted to look over such reaches of green meadows. The maples were just putting forth their leaves, and their shadows fell across the broad walk with pleasant coolness. The old well, with its oaken bucket and moss-covered sweep, made a pretty picture in the foreground. And, when the sun showed his great

face above the horizon, Alice wondered how any one
who could live in the country, and see such royal pictures every day, would choose the hot city, with its
endless restlessness, and "noise of many feet."

She left the door open, and the slant sunbeams
fell into the old kitchen, lighting up the huge fire-
place and the great pine table.

Every thing there was as neat and spotless as pains-
taking could make it; for Content had scoured the
tables to the last degree of brightness, and rubbed
the tin until it shone like silver. Alice could see
nothing to be improved here. Then she passed on
to the sitting-room. She tried to imagine how the
sight of it would affect her aunt and cousins, —
would they appreciate all the efforts that had been
made for their comfort? There were the pretty
cane-seat chairs, and the neat crimson carpet, covered
with flecks of sunshine which streamed through the
half-open blinds Alice had admired so much. Her
aunt's favorite work-table stood in the corner; and
choice vases, shells, and pictures ornamented the
mantel. If the room could have been improved, it
must have grown brighter beneath the look of loving satisfaction Alice cast upon every thing. Just
as Content came down into the kitchen, Alice surprised her by darting like a young fawn through the
open door, out upon the lawn beneath the maples;
and, before she had done wondering what could be
"de matter wid de dear chile," she came back,

her arms filled with flowering lilacs, sprigs of hyacinth, and English violets.

"See, Content, I am going to fill the vases. Don't you think it will make the room look more cheerful?"

"You done get a death o' cold, Miss Alice. Jest look at dem sleeves!"

"Oh! it don't hurt me, Content. What are you going to have for breakfast?"

Content was innocent of an idea, and declared she would get any thing Alice ordered.

"What is there in the house, Content?"

"Not much 'count of any thing, honey. Massa Whiting done got few tings, an' say he be back pretty soon."

"Well, Content, you may get what you like for breakfast, and I will go and arrange for dinner. Do you know, Content, that they will be here by noon? We must be sure and have a good dinner." She turned round, and saw Fred looking sadly at her.

"It's too bad, Alice, for you to be worried about such trifles."

"A pretty substantial trifle, however," she replied, with a brightening smile. "Come, Fred, I am going to press you into the service, and get you to draw some water from the old well."

Fred made a wry face, but went, — so hard is it for us to yield inclination to duty.

The old stage was sweeping slowly round the bend. Mrs. Whiting leaned out to look at the house her husband pointed out. "See there, Emily," said. he, "some friends of mine live there; don't you think it is a pretty place?"

"What do you mean, William? I hope you don't know anybody here. I'm sure I don't want to make any acquaintances."

"No: such society is not proper for genteel people, who have been used to the highest circles," said Lizzie scornfully.

"You will find, my daughter, that pride sometimes drinks from the same cup with disappointment. That is our home."

"And there is Alice at the door," said Ada.

"And so that's where we're to be buried alive, is it?" said Mrs. Whiting petulantly, as she threw herself back on the seat.

"That's where I hope we shall be buried away from the follies of fashionable life, Emily."

The kiss which Alice received from her uncle ought to have satisfied any reasonable demand of affection; and Alice was satisfied. With expectant eagerness she led them into the cozy sitting-room, and relieved them of their heavy travelling apparel.

"I believe I shall like it," said Ada, when she had taken a survey of the room. "Why, Alice, where did you pick up that white apron and pink ribbon? You look like a rosebud, poetically speaking."

"Just like you, Ada," said Lizzie. You like every thing for five minutes. You never would have been fit for society, even if we had not lost our property. You have a shocking *mauvais gout.*"

"I think it is a little bird's-nest of a home," said Alice. "Mother used to say it needed only a happy home and a contented heart to make up the sum of human enjoyment."

"Remember who you are talking to," said Fred. "Our guests are leaders of the *ton*, and with them such things as hearts are obsolete articles."

The table had been set with the utmost care, and Alice had endeavored to arrange it so that her aunt and uncle would miss nothing to which they had become accustomed. Even Mrs. Whiting's face lost some of its gloominess, when she saw the care and taste which had been bestowed upon every thing.

The afternoon was a busy one for all. Mr. Whiting went over the farm once more, and speculated upon its resources.

His wife abandoned herself to the headache and her sofa, declaring that she had no doubt that her ride in that clumsy old stage would make her sick for a week.

Even our old friend Sam busied himself in making himself comfortable. He honored the kitchen with his presence, much to the annoyance of Content. There he sat on the huge wood-box, his legs dangling over the sides, and his great hands hanging awkwardly out of his short jacket sleeves. He was furiously whittling a pine stick, and every now and then winking and glancing provokingly at Content..

" I say, "Tent, jest you guess what I'm making of this 'ere."

"Dunno. I reckon I kin 'tend to my own 'fairs," replied Content, with haughty displeasure.

" Wall, seein' as its a friend, I guess I'll tell ye. I've jest got tired o' seein' you wear them cotton handkerchiefs, an' so I'm makin' you a wooden comb to hold up the tresses, as Liz says. I say 'Tent," he added, with another leer, " why didn't you have white wool ? Its a mighty sight cleaner-lookin' than black."

" Sam ! " said Alice sternly, coming into the room just as he dodged a blow from Content's weighty palm.

He was still in a moment, and stood with open eyes and mouth, staring at her, as if she had been an apparition. Her voice only had an influence over him, and he almost dropped the knife from his hand in his sudden surprise.

" Have you done all the chores, Sam ? "

" I guess so," he answered sheepishly.

" Have you sawed the wood, as Uncle William told you ? "

" I done jest so, miss."

" And washed the carryall, and fed the horse ? "

"I guess like enough."

"Then go, and leave Content, if you cannot stay here without troubling her." Sam went, glad to escape from Alice's eye, which seemed to read his falsehood through and through.

"Gorry!" said he, drawing a long breath, "I didn't jist mean to tell that. I guess it comes natural like for me to lie. But I didn't say yes or no to either one or t'other."

To show his remorse, Sam performed his duties immediately.

Alice gave Content some necessary orders, and then went up to her room to rest awhile. But the busy brain would not let her sleep. She puzzled over problems too difficult for her to solve. This life they had commenced, would it be a happy one? Her uncle knew nothing about farming. He had no income. How were they to live? She started at her own thoughts, thinking that she had been questioning of matters over which she had no control; and she resolved she would no longer distress herself with such gloomy forebodings.

Little did the family dream, as time passed on, of the cares and responsibility which Alice took upon herself, — little of the petty vexations which were mastered by her patience. Content knew absolutely nothing of domestic economy. She conducted the cooking with her usual extravagance. And all Alice's eloquence was required to give her an idea of the altered circumstances of the family.

The arrangement of the table devolved on Alice also. She was scrupulous that no change should be perceived here. How differently each one regarded her as she performed these little household duties! Fred would look at her sadly, wondering at that cheerful patience which he could not understand; yet contenting himself the while in a state of half apathy, too much occupied with his own misfortunes to think of being of any active use.

Spring lengthened into summer. The farm had been well stocked, and, with the help of a reliable, practical hired man, and Mr. Whiting's scientific knowledge, well cultivated. But pride and idleness are poor inmates of a farm-house. If willing hands had joined to make each burden light, there would have been some hope of happy success. As it was, the cost of the family was great, — more than all Mr. Whiting could realize from his land. Alice sighed to herself, as she watched the lines of his face growing deeper and deeper. He was working too hard, that was plain; but never a word of complaint passed his lips. Mrs. Whiting thought herself aggrieved in having to live out of the world, and spent her time either in fashionable indolence or useless embroidery. "It was natural," she said, "for Alice to like house-work; she had been born to it. It was as natural

9*

for her to handle the broom as for Lizzie to play the piano."

It was a hot August evening. The air had been somewhat cooled by a heavy shower, and every leaf and twig glittered in the moonbeams. Alice walked back from the old kitchen door, where she had been gazing out, recalling old memories, and took a seat in the sitting-room. Her heart was softened, and her eyes heavy with unshed tears.

Mr. Whiting leaned his head upon his hand despondingly. "Wife," said he, "I believe we shall have to curtail."

"How, for mercy's sake?" said the lady dryly.

"I don't know, I am sure," he replied; "but it must be done. There's the land hardly will bring me in any thing. It won't more than support us, letting alone selling any thing."

"But there's the railroad stock," suggested Mrs. Whiting.

"A dead loss almost," replied her husband. "It wont probably bring more than twenty cents on a dollar."

"Oh, dear!" groaned the lady. "William, what do you trouble me with these petty things for? And my health so miserable!"

Alice could see the fire flash into her uncle's eyes, and then die out again in his effort for self-control.

"Do you find it so hard to hear them, Emily?

What would you do if you had to meet and bear them ? "

" Goodness knows, it would kill me ! I am almost dead now. I miss my maid so much. I was thinking only yesterday I would ask you to send to the city for one."

" Impossible, Emily. I tell you these money cares are tightening their grasp upon me every day. Unless something comes to relieve me, we shall be completely ruined."

" We are that now," said his wife. " We couldn't be worse off."

Mr. Whiting thought very bitterly of what worse thing might come, but said nothing.

Lizzie, Ada, and Fred talked apart. Lizzie was eloquent in praise of a new acquaintance named Henri Claremont. She declared she had not seen such style and grace since she left New York ; while Fred protested that he was a humbug, and told his sister that if he had set his net for flies he wouldn't take up with a gnat. Lizzie said he had promised to call upon her soon. But she did not tell Fred that she had allowed her new friend to believe her father was an odd old gentleman, very rich, who lived in the country during the warm season.

Mr. Whiting did not seem to hear any thing. He still sat looking dreamily upon the floor. Alice went over to his chair, and laid her hand upon his arm.

"Uncle William, perhaps, — I meant to say, maybe *I* might do something!"

Mr. Whiting smiled incredulously, but drew Alice nearer. "You have heard the story of the poor prisoner," said he, "whose dungeon walls drew nearer and nearer every day until they crushed him. I am just such a prisoner."

"No, uncle; for you have hope."

"It is a forlorn hope, child."

"Dear uncle," said Alice, putting her arm around his neck, "you know poor help is better than none; and oftentimes the weakest hand may raise a burden. I am going to tell you my plan. Miss Newton has offered me a situation as assistant in the seminary. Now, uncle, you know it will not take a great deal of my time; besides, I love to teach, and should like to help you. It will not be much, to be sure; but it shall all be yours."

Mr. Whiting's face grew strangely agitated. Strong passion was there, touched with kindly sympathy and love, as if the depths of that manly soul were being broken up, and the faith which still lay deeply underlying it were streaming out, glorifying the face, till it shone with peaceful beauty. Alice had never seen him look so before.

"My own little Alice," he said, "where will your self-sacrifice end? Truly God has blest me more than I deserve. I know it all, my child. May God bless you!"

" What is it you mean, uncle ? " said Alice, with filling eyes.

" I mean, Alice, that I was poor, and now am rich ; for I have found a gratèful and unselfish child. Mrs. Cushing told me all. So you love your Uncle William well enough to give up wealth and ease to live with him in poverty."

How is it, that sometimes a thrill of electric sympathy will pass from soul to soul through the medium of a single word ? Mr. Whiting stretched out his arms, and Alice came to them, and said softly, with a soulful look, " Uncle." But in that one word was expressed patience and hope and an earnest love.

" Alice," said he, when they had sat silent for some time, " what prevented you from going with Mrs. Cushing ? "

" Duty."

" Who told you your duty ? "

" I asked of our Father a knowledge of the right way."

" Why don't he tell me *my* duty, Alice ? "

" Don't you know his words, uncle ? — ' Every one that asketh receiveth.' "

" But why don't he show us the right, so that none could go astray ? He could make us what he would, and compel us to do right."

" I don't know, uncle. I suppose he means that we should earn the gifts he sends. Our virtues would not be of so much value to us if God gave them without our working."

" So then you have earned your virtues, Alice ? " said Mr. Whiting; with a return of his natural playfulness. " But, Alice, you told me once that self-denial was duty, and only in duty could we find happiness. Now, can we be happy to be always warring against our own natures? and can God be good to require it of us ? "

Alice looked distressed. She did not like to parade her knowledge, yet she longed to convince her uncle of the truth of that gospel he held so lightly.

" Dear Uncle William, I am a child, almost. Pray read for yourself. No one can do His work till they have learned to love Him."

" But, Alice," said Mr. Whiting, eager to know the reason of her faith, " I have never seen God, and how can I love him? We love our friends because we see them before us, and we are always working for them, and they for us ; and we can tell them of our love."

Was it the soft ray of moonlight which stole in at the open door which gave that uplifted face such a brightness, or was it the inner light of a great truth ?

" That is just the reason we love Him, Uncle William, because he is working for us, and we for him. When we open our eyes, and are willing to trust him, then he sends his light to show us the work he has given us to do. O uncle! is it not a glorious thought that we can be co-workers with him? that in the great world we may give help to His children, if it be but a cup of cold water to a disciple? And don't we — wouldn't you — love a being who is all light and perfection, even if we cannot see him? He is the vision of our own souls. The more we love and hope and trust, the higher and purer we shall view God, the nearer we shall be like him."

She hung her head, abashed, like a startled fawn, and then stole one glance at her uncle's face. He was looking intently at her, half awed by the force and power of her words. They were sitting alone in the room, and the candle had burned to that socket, but through the shimmering moonlight Alice thought she saw a tear on his face. She slipped from his arms, and he released her without a word. He seemed to have lost all thought of her in the greatness of the thought she had left him.

Oh! how near to us all lie the gates of the Hereafter of Light! Mr. Whiting's soul lay in the dark shadow of unbelief; but the hand of a girl had turned it backward, and given him a glimpse of the inner glory. Alice would have been frightened, had she known the extent of her influence over her uncle. Perhaps she had indeed given a cup of cold water to a thirsty soul.

Long after Alice lay wrapped in peaceful slumber, Mr. Whiting paced to and fro in the desolate sitting-room. He was studying that great problem of life, which, once solved, gives us the key to a wider and a better future. He saw men and the world as a shadow, a past dream, and himself standing alone, — a soul to be drawn upward into that good which he dimly comprehended as a light streaming down from above; and through all the dream the form of Alice seemed floating upward with beckoning finger, till she was lost in the brightness.

CHAPTER XXIII.

"Can you fasten my horse anywhere here, boy?" said a tall, foreign-looking gentleman, as he alighted at the farm-house steps.

Sam, lost in amazement at this sudden apparition of gentility, stood silent, with open eyes and mouth, regarding the stranger with curious coolness.

The gentleman repeated his question.

"Guess you don't belong round here anywhere, do you? From New York, mebbe?" said Sam, answering the question by asking another in true Yankee fashion.

His listener turned haughtily away, and ascended the steps, while Sam proceeded to tie the horse in the most awkward manner, by putting a rope round his neck, and then fastening it to a post. And just as Lizzie, all smiles and bows, came down to meet her visitor, Sam was dancing round the post, full of mischief and joy at having tied a knot which no mortal but himself could undo.

Henri Claremont was a gentlemanly looking person, tall and dark complexioned; and altogether such a one as would be likely to attract any young girl who loved show and romance and knightly manners. In dress he was faultless; and his honied speech and flattering attentions, it could be plainly seen, had given him a large place in Lizzie's favor. His dark hair fell in jetty ringlets around his neck; and a spotless collar, turned over *a la* Byron, gave him an air of jaunty freedom not at all unbecoming.

Alice had been at work in her garden, and as she came in at the back door caught a glimpse of the visitor. Hastily putting off her gardening gloves, she went into the kitchen.

"Content, what are you going to have for dinner? We shall have company."

Content raised her eyebrows curiously, and said she was going to have hashed meat.

Alice smiled. "What else have you in the house, 'Tenty? Couldn't you make one of those French puddings we used to have? You have plenty of eggs, haven't you?"

"Heaps on 'em."

Alice threw on her sunbonnet, and, taking the egg-basket from its peg, went out to hunt eggs among the old roads and haymows. The basket hung lightly upon her arm, — so lightly that she forgot its presence, and began thinking about past scenes and old friends and happy egg-huntings of long ago. The hot summer sun looked down on ripening grain and mellow fruit, the air was vocal with the hum of insects; and Alice's heart warmed with happy feeling like the summer glow of nature. A sense of perfect rest came over her, — a feeling of great freedom. She was in the open fields, with only the sky overhead; there was nothing to bind her. Was she not a child again? The sweet clover blossoms looked up at her as they did when she wove chaplets of their white and red blooms; the birds sang the same old tunes. Was she not the same little child who once made the fields her playground, and the birds and flowers her companions? So Alice thought, until her brow grew serious as she realized how far she had travelled from the trusting confidence of childhood. Ah! the childish brook becomes the deep river of womanhood; the waters which gushed so free then have now learned the rocks and shallows of the life-stream, and their singing is softened into a deep and serious murmur.

So Alice thought as she sauntered on through the garden gate. "I am a woman indeed," said she aloud. "I have learned to be prudent, worldly, where once I only loved and confided. And·yet the Word says, ' Except ye become as little children, ye shall in no wise enter into the kingdom of heaven.' "

She repeated the text over and over again as she passed along, meditating upon its beautiful simplicity. A voice aroused her.

" Miss Morton, may I have the pleasure of carrying your basket ? "

The basket served as a link between the past and present. Alice recollected herself, and became suddenly aware that a pair of brown eyes were looking intently on her face.

"Thank you, Mr. Hall," she answered with some embarrassment. "I believe my thoughts have literally run away with me. I came out to hunt eggs, and have thought myself away out here."

"Yes," said he, taking her basket with a grave look, "I believe I shall have to arrest you for trespassing. Did you know that this is father's meadow?"

"No, I did not. You will not enforce the law where there is ignorance of it," said Alice playfully.

"I am afraid I shall in this case. I want you to walk up to the house with me. Come, will you not?"

"Not to-day, Mr. Hall."

"But do you know our family think it very strange you come to see us so seldom? Father talks about it nearly every day."

"It seems, then, that the old adage, 'out of sight out of mind,' does not hold good here. I am glad I have so many good friends."

"You have a great many, I am sure," said Edward, in a tone that made Alice uncomfortable, it was so very significant.

Edward declared himself perfectly at leisure, and in love with the romantic business of egg-hunting. The basket was full to the brim; and they had almost reached the farm gate, when Edward, turning his face towards her, wistfully said, —

"Will you not be kind enough to tell me how you understand the passage you were repeating when I met you?"

Alice remembered blushingly that she had been thinking aloud. She was silent.

"Forgive me if I ask too much," said Edward. "But I have been much troubled to find a satisfactory meaning to that phrase. Is it not our duty to help one another in the pursuit of truth?"

"I will not urge my ignorance and your wisdom, Mr. Hall; but, if my poor opinion can avail you, you shall have it. But, first, you must tell me where you think the kingdom of heaven is?"

"I have always considered it the scene of our future life, — the presence of God and his angels."

"Then my explanation will be vain. I do not so consider."

"Where do *you* think it is?" said Edward.

"Within you. We need not wait for a future world to be in the presence of God. Now this kingdom is promised not to the proud, but to the poor in spirit. The rich, the haughty, must humble themselves, must become as a child, before they can enter it. It was that I was thinking of this morning. How hard it is, with our trials, our experiences, our idols, to keep the heart open and pure, to still be meek and trustful as a child!"

"Is it possible to be that?" said Edward, in a low tone.

"Not without help: but the divine Alchemist can turn even selfishness to the pure gold of virtue; and the failing props of the world teach us faith and childlike trust in our Father. That is the way I understand it. Doubtless it is a childish way." ,

"The very reason why it should be the best way," said Edward. "Thank you, Miss Morton. You have rendered me no common service. I never seemed to realize it before."

He declined entering the house, but stood at the gate, watching her, till she was out of sight in the turnings of the path.

"Truly," said he to himself, "of such is the kingdom of heaven."

"What a pity," thought Alice, "that such a noble student leaves out of his library the best of all works!"

The dinner proved to be all that was expected, with the addition of some fine trout, the product of Fred's morning sport. Mr. Whiting looked serious; and Fred's brow was ominously overcast at sight of their visitor. He conducted himself, as Lizzie said, with "graceful elegance;" though Ada and Alice both thought his manners a little affected. Mr. Whiting talked with Lizzie a long time after his departure. He saw too late his failure in duty, and endeavored to atone for it by grave and earnest counsel and fatherly advice. Lizzie listened wearily, as if she thought it all very dull, and assured her father repeatedly that she cared nothing for Henri Claremont, save as a friend and a fashionable acquaintance. Still her father left her with a heavy heart.

And so week after week passed away, and Autumn was drawing near. The fields stood yellow with golden corn, the orchards were dropping with golden fruit. A comfortable home they had, with every immediate necessity ; but those numberless little wants, which only money can supply, were lacking. The fashionable garments were replaced by the plainest home-made goods. Even Mrs. Whiting, seeing how her husband and children exerted themselves, seemed roused to a feeling of interest, and used her needle to better advantage than in embroidery. But, for all this, the winter was approaching. The family was large, and Alice saw with anxiety that her uncle grew paler, and more thoughtful than ever.

From time to time she heard from Ellen Lee. Rumor said she was a " splendid teacher," who was in herself a demonstration of the great law of kindness. Charles was still in Italy, filling out copies of great pictures for American gentlemen, and enriching his mind by the study of the noblest artists. Every word which Alice dropped concerning his success and genius made Fred sigh, and put him into a profound revery.

The warm rays of the September sun stole in through the open door, and streamed across the sitting-room. Fred sat and looked dreamily at Alice, as, with the sunshine playing round her fingers, she stitched nimbly away at her work, moving her lips at intervals, as if to recall a lost passage or forgotten text.

"What are you doing, Cousin Alice?"

"Nothing very romantic, Fred. I am mending a stocking."

"But I should think, when a stocking came to that pass, it was time it was thrown away."

"Perhaps so, for rich folks like you," said Alice, with a curious smile; "but we must either patch them or take the other alternative."

"What is that?"

"Wearing them with holes in them."

Fred drummed his foot on the floor, and said nothing, though Alice felt sure a storm of feeling would succeed the calm. It came at last.

"It's a shame, Alice, — a downright shame, — for people to be so fettered by poverty. Just the lack of a few dollars, that we would have thrown away a year ago. There is no chance for either of us ever doing any thing or being anybody. I say there's no comfort in such a life." And Fred got up and walked with rapid strides around the room.

"No comfort, perhaps, but much healthful discipline."

"But who wants to be disciplining for ever. It may benefit you, but it don't me one bit."

"You do not know yourself, Cousin Fred. You are not the same being now that you were one year ago."

"That's a fact. I am minus money, prospects, friends, and every thing else."

Alice said nothing, preferring to let this morbid feeling expend itself. He stopped in his walk, and came and looked over her shoulder. A German grammar lay open upon her lap.

"Pray, are you studying and sewing at the same time? I do not believe there ever was such perseverence."

"Oh, yes! Do you forget Charlotte Brontë, learning her German with her grammar elevated above the kneading-trough?"

Fred shut his lips tightly, determining for once to control himself. Finally he drew an ottoman to Alice's side, and looked up gravely into her face. "Do not think I have not seen your anxiety and father's embarrassment, — they have sunk deep into my heart; and now I think for me to stay here longer would be almost a crime. I am going away, Alice. Judge Hall has offered to place me in a law-office in New York. So I shall give up my hopes of college, and study hard for excellence. Edward strongly urged this course; and the judge said the best college was the world, and the highest

10

diploma a noble countenance, written by God's own hand in lines of truth and honor."

Fred's face shone with the old generous light. No one would have called him moody or passive then. Alice looked thoughtful; and, when she answered, she spoke indirectly, —

"Fred, you are richer than you ever were before. You are willing to go into life, and take honor and integrity for your companions. Thank God, my dear cousin, that your loss has proved gain; and that it came before flattery had enervated you, or conceit wholly robbed you of manly truth and honor."

CHAPTER XXIV

FASHIONABLE EDUCATION.

AND so Fred went to the law-office, and Alice entered the seminary at the beginning of the next quarter. She might have missed the society of her sprightly cousin, had not new duties occupied every thought, and new faces awakened her interest. The young children at the seminary learned to love her, as indeed did all who came within her influence. But, most of all, the childish confidence of Nina Hall endeared her to the heart of her young teacher. She was Nina's oracle, — every thing she said or did was perfect in Nina's eyes ; and she would sit for hours gazing upon Alice's face, with a mingled look of love and reverence, watching her as she told the children of nature or of God.

Not unfrequently Nina would come to school with her hands filled with autumn flowers, — sometimes her own gift, and sometimes from " Brother Edward." And not seldom did Edward manage to stray out of his way, though these strayings always brought him to the seminary gate at the close of the session.

We have not mentioned Ada since the failure. It is because her heart and mind have been so steadily improving. She needed no attention. Ada's mind always followed the leadings of the strongest influence around it. Once she had yielded to Lizzie's flattery and folly; now Alice had regained her power over her, and almost moulded her anew. It is a misfortune of such minds that they are so impressible. They are like the water, which is mobile and limpid of itself, but which will take the form of any vessel which contains it. Happy was it for Ada that a good and pure life was being worked out before her, that she might shape her conduct after its excellent virtues. Lizzie looked on scornfully when Ada listened to Alice's "preaching," as she called it. Ah! there was no danger of Lizzie. Her education had been too complete to allow of change.

October began to drop its golden leaves upon the brown earth, and the nuts had opened in the forests. The farm-house doors no longer stood open all day long, but only unclosed to admit the warm afternoon sunshine. On one of these warm afternoons, the gentleman with the foreign air descended the farm-house steps, and sought his horse, which as usual Sam had tied in a double-and-twisted Yankee knot. Just as Sam dodged a blow from the heavy riding-whip, a paper fluttered down, and fell at the horse's feet.

"What are you stooping there for, you rascal?"

"I jest wanted to see if that hoss's hoofs wan't gettin' rusty!"

The paper was safe in Sam's pocket. Half an hour had not elapsed ere Sam saw the stranger coming rapidly down the road.

"Here, you little rascal!" said he, vaulting off his horse. "Have you seen any thing of a piece of white paper?"

Sam gave a spring, and alighted astride the farm fence, and eyed the stranger very coolly. "Why, have you lost one?"

"I don't choose to converse with menials," he replied, with dignity. "Answer me, — yes or no."

"Well," said Sam, "mebbe yes, and 'mebbe no. Seems to me I did see suthin' like a scrap o' paper. 'Twan't very white, though."

"Where is it? — give it to me," said the other eagerly.

"I don't know. Didn't say's I did, did I?"

Sam suddenly turned a somersault, and landed in a ball on the grass, out of reach of the stranger's whip. Henri Claremont turned his horse angrily, but soon returned again, urged by some mysterious impulse.

"Here, you boy," said he. "If you don't tell me where that paper is, I'll have you cut up by inches, and skinned alive."

Coming close up to the fence, though still cautiously avoiding the whip, Sam said, in a low, confidential tone, "Supposin' now, stranger, you was a gentleman, and I was another, and you should give me that gold ring on your finger, and I should give you that paper, — only supposin', — would ye do it ? "

At first the stranger only seemed beside himself with indignation at the fellow's impudence. But his desire for the paper overcame every thing else; and he promised the ring, which Sam, with true Yankee spirit, demanded and received first. He then searched in his long trousers' pocket, and drew up a piece of soiled and crumpled paper, which he put into the stranger's hand.

" This isn't the one I want. The one I want has writing on it."

" Guess I haven't seen that one. I happened to see this stickin' up in the grass, and thought mebbe it might be yourn." And Sam, with the ring on his finger, and the real paper safe in his pocket, disappeared in the shrubbery at the back of the house, leaving his angry and discomfited friend to digest his rage as best he might.

About a week after the above occurrence, as Alice returned through the twilight of the now chilly evening, she encountered Sam, who seemed desirous of speaking to her. She spoke kindly to him, and Sam answered respectfully that he had "suthin' to give her," and, bringing up the stranger's paper, put it into her hand.

" You see, Miss Alice," said he, — using the respectful language common to him when speaking to

her, — " I've had this scrap o' paper more'n a week.
I picked it up in the grass as I was ontying the
stranger's horse. He was awfully consarned about
it ; and I haint had no luck since I took it. The
grindstone broke down ; and I fell off the horse and
like to break my neck; and it's taken the butter
more'n twice as long to come 'n it ever did afore. So
I'm jest goin' to give it to you. I couldn't make out
a word of it. Mebbe you'd tell me ? " he added, his
curiosity once more getting the better of his awe of
Alice.

Alice took the paper and unfolded it. It was
dirty and greasy, having been so long in Sam's
pocket, in company with knives, top-cords, ginger-
bread, and the like. It was a letter written in a
fine French hand, and commenced abruptly without
any address. Before Alice had read far, she became
aware that the contents of that paper ought not to
be seen by her eye ; but statements of such startling
nature were set forth there, that she read on over two
pages of note-paper, and finally read the name
signed to it, without fairly comprehending where
she was, what she was doing, or what the paper
really contained. She read it a second time, and
then her mind took in all the force and power of the
writer's words. It purported to come from the wife
of Eugene Lovering, and was filled with the com-
plaints of a despairing and much-wronged woman.
It accused him of neglect, of failure to meet

promises, and finally charged him with changing his name to Henri Claremont, and stated that rumor coupled his name with a beautiful Miss Whiting. There were vague hints also of a forgery and pursuit, and an earnest prayer that he would escape before it was too late. The name signed was simply " Evelina."

The blush of shame and indignation rose to Alice's cheeks. Totally unconscious of all save the astounding revelations of this letter, Alice walked into the house and up to her room. There, as usual with her, she fell into a fit of profound musing. She thought over every thing connected with Henri Claremont's acquaintance in the family. Could it be possible that they had allowed such a viper to creep among them, and perhaps to poison the mind of Lizzie with falsehood .and flattery? He who could be so dead to truth and honor in one case could be in another. Alice knew Lizzie to be a romantic girl, whose mind rested on no firm foundation of principle; but she knew that her pride would scorn one like Henri Claremont. Nor was she mistaken. Yet Lizzie's lack of prudence would have prevented her seeing him in his true colors. She had never questioned the motives or pretensions of others. She gave admiration and respect to a glittering outside, and a ready ear to her own praise. Hence Alice feared. She knew Lizzie's haughty temper, and that she would never ask or listen to advice from others. She thought of her cousin in the presence of one without honor or integrity, and shuddered. As little as Alice knew of romance or day-dreaming, she could readily see how easily one of Lizzie's unstable mind might be allured like a child by an empty promise or a goodly seeming. But here was this note! She had no right to keep it in her possession, and yet to whom could she give it?   Fred was away; her aunt's nerves rendered her unfit for any emergency ; and Ada was inefficient as a child. No ! She felt that she must go to her uncle. As Lizzie's father, it was most proper he should look after the interests of his child.

Mr. Whiting sat in the twilight of the old kitchen mending a rake. As Alice came in with her usual quiet, he raised his head with a smile, and asked her some questions about her school. He had finished getting in his harvest that day, and dismissed his hired man ; and now he was feeling a little discouraged about the future. Alice thought to herself that it was a poor time to trouble him with unpleasant intelligence. She arose and procured a light; and then going to her uncle's side said, " Uncle William, you are not feeling very well, are you ? "

" Not so well as I ought, with so many good comforters around me. But, Alice, you look pale. I shall forbid your teaching altogether."

" It isn't the labor that makes me pale, uncle, but only a little sad thought. I have learned some un-

10*

pleasant facts to-day, which I meant to make known
to you. I did not think to see you so sad and
weary. Shall I tell you now, or wait till to-
morrow ? "

Mr. Whiting looked alarmed, and begged her to
tell him immediately. And Alice, who saw that he
would be tormenting himself with vague fears, if
she delayed, put the note into his hand, with the
story of its discovery.

There is no point on which a man is more deli-
cately sensitive than that of family honor. Poverty,
loss of friends, even death itself, can be better borne
than disgrace. Mr. Whiting had supposed that the
opinion of the world was nothing to him, that in
him the fires of ambition were gone out. He was
mistaken. The fires of pride had indeed been
dashed out by the cold water of misfortune, but beneath they still smouldered; and in that hour the
thought of what the world would say was strong
within him. That his spotless name should be
spoken abroad in the same breath with the name of
a forger! That his daughter should be thought
of at the same time with one so utterly worthless!
That he should have harbored beneath his roof a
felon! It was too much! Forgive him, if, as he
walked nervously to and fro, some bitter words
crossed his lips! Forgive him, ye fashionable
mothers and exquisite daughters, if in that moment
he hurled terrible denunciations at your pet theories

of education, and spoke some bitter truths of his daughter's folly and imprudence ! It was natural.

Alice raised her head. She could not bear to see him so. She arose and laid her hand on his arm, — "Uncle William, Lizzie was more sinned against than sinning."

" True, — too true, alas ! " he said. " I have sinned against her cruelly. It is not her fault. It is mine."

Alice was silent.

" O Alice ! " he faltered, " how nearly I had been the ruin of my child ! "

Still Alice said nothing. The sight of her uncle's deep humiliation weighed upon her. The tears rushed to her eyes, and she pressed his hand in sympathy. Looking up, he saw her weeping.

" O Alice ! " he faltered, — " little Alice, if all the world were like you, we should have no need of guardian angels. Had it not been for my foolish weakness, my daughters might have been like you. But God is just. 'He that soweth the wind must reap the whirlwind.' I am punished. His judgments have fallen upon me very bitterly."

" God is merciful," whispered Alice.

" Yes, merciful ! " repeated Mr. Whiting. " My pride is broken like a reed, that I might acknowledge his hand. Perhaps some day I may say, 'Our Father,' as I did at my mother's knee."

The light burned dimly. The dark walls of the

old kitchen threw shadows into the room, which fell like a mantle over the bowed man. It was a strange unfolding of human life for one so young as Alice.

"May the Lord bless you, my dear uncle, and forgive us all our heart-wanderings!" and Alice was gone, leaving him alone with the night and his accusing thoughts.

Not with anger, but with a sad tenderness, did Mr. Whiting talk to his eldest daughter the next day. He pictured to her the evil of allowing every one indiscriminatingly to her acquaintance, who came with no stronger recommendation than a foreign style and fine coat. He talked lovingly and earnestly to her ; and the proud girl was softened, and some natural tears gave proof that the springs of right feeling were not entirely dried up. There are some minds which never apprehend danger till they are on the very verge of the precipice, — some who literally "take no thought of the morrow." Such was Lizzie Whiting. Her father realized that one so excitable, so thoughtless, needed all the checks of principle, and reflected sadly that the firm self-control and high culture which a true education would have given her had been thrown away by four years at a fashionable boarding-school.

The next week's papers from New York brought news that Eugene Lovering, *alias* Henri Claremont, had been arrested for forgery, and sentenced to the

State Prison for a long term of years. Lizzie shuddered as she read it.

"There is no safety for any one," said Ada.

"Yes," said Alice, "there is safety in a pure heart. A pure heart is a thermometer, and falls at every breath of evil. He who possesses this safeguard is rich, though he had nothing else."

Lizzie almost forgot herself. She was about to say, "O Alice! show me how to find this safeguard." But she checked herself. The good impulse was only the choked spring bubbling up amid the rubbish of a false life.

CHAPTER XXV

JUDGE HALL doated on his son,—that was plain; and no one blamed him for it. But "every heart knoweth its own bitterness;" and Judge Hall found his in his son's skepticism. It was a barrier in the path his father had longed to see him tread. It prevented his usefulness; it darkened his life. Edward believed in God, and loved nature as God's work; but of living faith he knew nothing. His religion was scientific,—built of philosophic theories and logical deductions, which his reason approved. And yet, beneath all, this high soul longed after truth, as the hart panteth for the water-brooks, and loathed the husks it fed on. But the stern pride of the man was there. He would not believe until reason and judgment approved; and so he crushed back the glowing aspirations of youth as a weakness. But there come times to all such souls, when they feel how poor a teacher is intellect alone. They realize that their fine words and lofty dreamings are more truly *lived out* every day by some lowly follower of Christ. They feel that they are like the fig-tree which bore only leaves.

Such a monitor was Alice Morton to Edward Hall. Circumstances had thrown them together much; and every conversation but revealed more fully her calm faith, her Christian principle. In vain Edward reasoned with himself, that she believed blindly; that she had never studied philosophy to any depth. The fact still remained, that she lived a truer life, — did more good, and was happier.

It was a dull day, — the first of December. Sam had brought Alice in the chaise to give her customary lesson to Nina, — a task which was a delight to her, for the child really had genius, and entered into the very soul of music. As Nina ran out of the room at the close of the hour allotted, Edward begged to be favored with some music. Alice's hands trembled some as she ran them over the keys. She had much rather have been excused; but she would not deny so simple a wish. She sang some pretty Scotch ballads, and some of Moore's charming songs. When about to rise, Edward said, "Pray, Miss Morton, favor me with one hymn, — that beautiful one, 'Jesus, lover of my soul.'"

For years that hymn had not passed Alice's lips. It was her mother's favorite. She touched the keys with unsteady fingers, and her voice trembled with suppressed feeling, — almost melted to tears. The memory of that sweet voice, which once sang it in her childish ears, was all Alice thought of; and she threw into it a depth of pathos and tenderness born of real feeling. As she sang the last beautiful verse, her voice almost failed her; but she choked back her tears, though her voice spoke them in the strain, —

> "Other refuge have I none, —
>   Hangs my helpless soul on Thee:
> Leave, oh! leave me not alone, —
>   Still support and comfort me.
> All my hope on Thee is stayed;
>   All my help from Thee I bring.
> Cover my defenceless head
>   With the shadow of Thy wing."

Alice rose, and would have passed from the room; but Edward sprang eagerly forward. "Stay, Miss Morton, — will you not let me thank you? will you not let me ask you one question?"

Alice sat down on the music-stool.

"Forgive me, Miss Morton; but I am going to ask you a question, which perhaps you will think a strange one. There is a man," began Edward, "who has lived all his life in the midst of plenty and prosperity. He worships the beautiful, and loves the good, wherever he finds it. God gave him talents, and he might use them if he would. To him as to all the world comes the command, 'Arise, and work!' But he sits idle. He feels that if he works it is vanity, if he is idle it is vanity; that either way the labor of man ᴠprofiteth nothing. He believes in goodness, and would like to raise his fellow-men; but he sees no hope. The millennium to him is a beautiful dream, and man's regeneration a sublime idea, but impossible to be realized. What would you think of such a one, Miss Morton?"

Alice gazed full into his face,—it was very earnest. Could it be possible he spoke of himself?

"I should think," replied she, "that his mind was morbid; and, before he could help his fellows, he must recover his own health."

"I am the man," replied Edward, blushing. "I would give worlds, Miss Morton, for the faith your hymn expressed. You felt it; so did I. But my reason said, 'It is only an emotion,—it cannot be trusted.' What is it that gives *you* this trust?"

"It is a knowledge of my own weakness. We are offered this refuge in the love of God,—upon whom should we lean, if not on Infinity?"

"But, Miss Morton, you take this for granted. Intellect takes nothing for granted."

"We cannot find both question and answer entirely in ourselves," replied Alice. "We must have a starting-point."

"But why this necessity? I want to see the reason of faith."

Alice smiled. "'Except ye become,'—have you forgotten that passage. When you were a child, Mr. Hall, and learned the alphabet, did you think of asking why the first letter was 'A'? I should as soon think of asking that question as asking if we could be sure of the love of God. It is the centre of the soul itself. It must be so."

Edward was silent, — the words had struck home. She was not skilled in the philosophies of the schools ; but she had the living fire of truth in her words.

" Thank you, Miss Morton. You must think I am a strange person. But I want to hear with the simplicity of a child. No sacrifice of pride would be too great if I could win truth."

Once more Alice smiled. " You mistake yourself, Mr. Hall. Your very renunciation of pride is a worse pride. You come to the door of heaven, and knock, and think yourself worthy of an answer because you have made so great a sacrifice of intellectual pride. You think it a great sacrifice for the man to become a child."

Edward had never thought of it before ; but it was true, — his conscience told him so.

" After all," said Alice, " we must come down to first principles. Our beginning and our ending is mystery, — the world is vanity. Our only refuge is faith in God. The fraction of human knowledge, reduced to its lowest terms, resolves itself at last into a cypher. Without God, we are but a handful of dust. With faith in him, that dust becomes like the ashes of the phœnix, from which " life and immortality shall be brought to light."

Edward gazed upon her in awe, — nearly in revercnce. She had risen from the seat, and now stood with glowing cheeks, and an eye kindled by thought. It was a burst of natural eloquence. He said nothing, and Alice sunk upon the music-stool with painful embarrassment at having spoken so earnestly.

At last he said, " But, Miss Morton, what shall we believe? Transcendentalism is too dreamy. The dogmas of the church are too narrow. What shall we believe?"

She rose up once more, and stepped somewhat forward. "Love truth, and seek it, — but not in the creeds of the world. Much study is a weariness of the flesh. Let us hear the conclusion of the whole matter, — 'Fear God and keep his commandments; for this is the whole duty of man.'"

And, when Edward looked up, she was gone. But not soon died her words from his mind. They were food for thought for many days.

CHAPTER XXVI.

"One year ago!" Many things may happen in a year. The hopes of thousands may have been wrecked, and the light that shone for them may now be streaming on the upturned faces of others. Ah! there are few hearts which do not recall "one year ago" with some secret pangs! Some for whom its circle began or ended with a grave! Some who watch the old year out with shivering sadness, because the warm fires of love have died out on their own hearthstones! And there are some who rejoice, because they have "fought a good fight, and travelled a sabbath day's journey nearer the celestial city."

"I am dead to the world," said Mr. Whiting on this Christmas Eve.

Do you remember Mr. Whiting's last Christmas Eve? Perhaps you can recall, as I do, the dreary drawing-room, the dying fire, the lonely man, and the sweet monitor — half woman, half child — who stood there with a lesson for him, which he began to learn from that time. But that was one year ago. Mr. Whiting's name is now no longer known on 'Change. The spacious halls have narrowed to the cozy rooms of the old-fashioned farm-house.

"We are very comfortable here, are we not, dear uncle?" said Alice, as they sat in front of the blazing wood fire. Her uncle assented with a gratified look. It reminded him of the family gatherings of his boyhood. The little sitting-room really shone. The bright blaze of the fire lit up the crimson carpet, and played in fantastic lights and shadows on the wall, and upon the happy faces of those assembled there.

"How pleasant it is!" said Ada. "Don't you think so, mother?" Mrs. Whiting sat apart in an easy-chair, and now raised her head languidly.

"Yes, dear," she answered, "for those who have known nothing better. Lizzie, do you remember Mrs. Hammersford's ball, last Christmas Eve?"

"Ah! never mind balls now, mother," said Fred, who had returned for the holidays. "We've got something better. Come, father, mother, Lizzie, Ada, look here!" and Fred threw open the door of the little library, from whence a stream of golden light fell merrily. There, blazing and flashing, stood a Christmas Tree. Fred and Alice and the girls looked roguish enough at the surprise they had caused the others. Fred would have Sam and Content called in. They came shyly from the kitchen, Sam gazing with admiring wonder. Few and simple were the gifts; but we love each other not so much for what is given as for the kindness of heart which prompts the offering. There was a

nice pair of slippers for Mr. Whiting, wrought by
Lizzie's willing fingers ; a handsome dress from Fred
for his mother ; a case of sketching pencils for Ada.
'Tenty was made extatic by the gift of another bandanna, gayer than the first ; and Sam was completely
overwhelmed by receiving for a gift what he had
long coveted, but never dreamed of possessing,—a
pair of patent-leather shoes, to replace a pair of old
clogs he had lost in the brook only a week before.
And was there nothing for Fred and Alice ?   Come
and look over Alice's shoulder, and we shall see.
She is standing at the bookcase, trying to see through
her tears a beautiful bound edition of the German
Poets.   Fred laughs, and shakes his head at her ex-
pressions of gratitude, and assures her that this gift
is nothing compared with the hair watch-guard he
holds in his hand.   " I shall always prize it, Alice,
as a memento of the three dear sisters I love."

Joyous was that Christmas Eve.   Hearts grew
warm with happy feeling, which had long been
frozen in the icy chains of fashion.   Some few
glimpses of household love had cheered them.   Mr.
Whiting felt that hére, at least, he could rest ; and
slowly the day-star was rising, in whose holy beams
was the promise of " Peace."   Only Mrs. Whiting
remained as ever, — restless, nervous, complaining.
All round the walls, bright holly-berries and ever-
greens had been hung.   The brown nuts that the
forest trees had given them were displayed for win-

ter cheer; and sober russets and golden pippins looked out temptingly from their beds of snowy corn.

"I am going to tell the name of your future spouse, Alice," said Fred, as he threw over her head a long apple-paring.

"A perfect 'E,' I declare," said Ada, as it curled up on the floor.

"Well, now for the last initial," laughed Fred. "I declare," said he, as it came down, "its an 'H.'"

"It looks more like an 'N,' I am sure," said the blushing Alice.

"No: it's a *bona fide* 'H,'" persisted her cousin. "It couldn't have been better, could it, Liz?" added he provokingly.

The soft rays of the study lamp fell across the library floor, and the judge sat among his law-papers, with dreamy eyes looking into the future, and back upon the past. Music and festivity had been there; for it was Christmas Eve. But now the dancing footsteps were hushed; the great clock in the hall pointed prayerfully to the hour of twelve, and the silver chimes rang out, as of old they did when the angels sang, "Glory to God in the highest; on earth peace, good-will towards men."

It was midnight,— the magic hour when, as old legends say, spirits walk the familiar places of the earth once more. And truly, as the light streamed over the gray hairs of that good old man, one might almost think a rewarding angel had circled his brow with its promised crown. It is a mistake to say that ·spirits walk the earth no more. They will walk with us, hand in hand, if our touch is pure and holy. They will sup with us and sojourn with us, if faith and' love are in our hearts and homes. They come to us now pure as when they came to Eden, trailing their white robes over the brown earth ; and where they stopped to comfort the earth-worm, or make a stained soul white again, we say the place is holy, and take off our shoes, and listen reverently, as if a voice should say, "Peace and good neighborhood."

A dark figure glided in with noiseless footfall, and stood by the old man's chair.

The old man smiles in his revery. He is think-ing, perhaps, of the many hearts he has made glad . in the past year ; and how the poor widow blessed him when he sent her food and fuel for a Christ-mas gift. But now his face darkens, his brow is troubled, and a tender sadness takes the place of the glad light in his eyes.

"Oh, my son! my son!" said the trembling lips.

The dark figure raised its head suddenly, and the judge started as if he heard a sigh.

"One thing have I desired of Thee above all others," said the judge prayerfully, — "that my son might come home to Thee and to me."

"Father, he has!" and, turning, the judge saw

his son standing with folded arms and compressed lips before him.

"It is Edward! it is my son!" said the judge, as he stretched out his arms; but Edward stood motionless.

"Father, I have sinned, and am not worthy of a blessing."

It is not for curious eyes to look upon the prodigal when he comes back to the arms of love. A calm joy, like the soft blessing of evening after a day of weary toil, settled around them. The struggle and the anxiety were over, and now they might rest in each other's love; while all around them flowed the golden band of that infinite love whose circle is Faith, and whose signet is Peace.

"The waves of life had no balm for me," said Edward, "till an angel went down before, and troubled the waters. Then I stepped in, and was healed."

"It is enough," said the judge. "My son is not an alien from the faith of his fathers."

CHAPTER XXVII.

"I TOLD you a story once, Miss Morton. Will you let me tell you another one?" asked Edward, as he drew his chair nearer hers.

Alice assented. She knew, that, when he told a story, it was worth listening to. Edward paused a moment, as if in thought, and then spoke as follows : " A young soul wandered out of the gate of Paradise. It hung its harp upon the willows that grow by the bank of the celestial river ; for the good Father said, 'Go work in my vineyard, and I will give thee a new harp, — even the heart of man, — that thou mayest attune it unto the melodies of love.' And so the white soul came into the world as a human child, with a divine gift. The angels of Truth and Peace were its elder sisters, and sang its first cradle-songs. Its face was not fair, as you would imagine the face of such a good spirit, but was dark, and some would say, at first sight, un- lovely. But, as she journeyed on, she played upon the magic harp ; and its tones were so sweet, that those who heard them said, 'An angel is passing,' and forgot her face in the softness of her song. By- and-by, the path became rugged and hard to tread. Then her feet began to falter, and her heart to grow somewhat heavy ; but, when every thing else had failed, this harp became all to her, and drew such sweet music from even the trial and trouble, that every one stood still to listen ; and as they listened their souls melted in them with longing after a life so true and beautiful as the song portrayed. For you remember the good Father had said she should attune the heart into the melodies of love.

" It came to pass, as she sojourned in a beautiful valley, that she met a brother soul, whose faith was destroyed by clouds of unbelief, — who had wasted his life, and had forgotten his God. The soul of the good monitor was stirred with pity. She touched her lyre, and the air rang out with a symphony so holy, so heavenly, that it seemed as if one might feel the very love of God of which she sang. And the young doubter, looking upward, saw light, and believed. He went his way ; but he could not forget the harp nor the maiden. He longed to hear the song once more, and gather faith from the lips of his monitor. Do you see the moral of my tale ? "

Alice blushed painfully. The point of the story had been too plain ; but she said nothing.

" This harp," continued Edward, " was the maiden's heart. Its silver strings were love, faith, patience, hope, meekness, and gentleness. Those around her always heard some harmony breathing through her lips. And I have heard it said that whoever should join hands with her for the life-journey would hear those sweet voices ever singing, and inherit the blessing she will receive when she goes back to her Father.   Look up, Alice, and tell me if I may hope for this guidance."

Alice's eyes were full of tears as she put her hand in Edward's.

CHAPTER XXVIII.

A JOYFUL REVELATION.

THE fading sunset of a soft June day was wrapping hill and valley in glory as Ellen Lee once more came back to her old home. She put her head out of the old stage window to note each familiar thing, — the spire of the seminary, glistening in the distance ; the slope of the green hill ; and the farm boys going home, or finishing their labor, with merry tune and whistle.

It was Ellen Lee ; but how changed ! The traces of deep sorrow were upon her face ; her brow was paler than ever ; and the soft bands of hair were parted smoothly on her forehead, instead of flying in truant ringlets as they did once. A suit of neat black had taken the place of the coarse homemade garments in which we last saw her. But the stage rolled on to the farm door, and brought Ellen to her old home and to a warm welcome. Alice and Ada embraced her with gladness; and Lizzie seemed interested in the young stranger, whose deep mourning dress seemed to call for sympathy and plead for kindness.

" She has a sweet face, has she not ? " said Mr. Whiting ; and his wife could not but assent.

" Charles and I are orphans, dear Alice," she

said, as they sat at the pleasant west window that
night. "They are both gone home, — mother, and
grandfather too. Sometimes I wish I were. But
I must stay while He gives me 'work to do. Alice,
if it had not been for you, I should have been a
misanthrope."

"No, dear Ellen, you would not: there is too
much good in you. You were only a little tired
and unhappy then. Now it is better, and you have
many friends."

"I have lost my best ones, Alice! Henceforth I
have marked out my life. I will be a true worker
in my Lord's vineyard. I will be like a tree, which
brings forth its fruit in due season. All the good
that I can yield shall be given up, lest at any time
the Lord of the vineyard should say, 'Lo! these
many years do I come seeking fruit, and finding
none. Cut it down.'"

"But what shall you do, Ellen?"

"Do you remember, Alice, a conversation we
once had upon duty? I then felt that my talent for
composition should be encouraged, and longed to
write rather than teach. That longing has never
left me. Now the way is open for the fulfilment of
my hopes. I am going to Italy. Brother Charles
has sent for his lonely sister to come and live with
him at Florence. So I shall go in the fall."

"I am glad," said Alice, pressing her hand. "I
knew the future had some good in store for you.

The last shall be first, and the first last," said she, with a sigh.

Ellen drew her chair nearer her friend. "Can you bear some startling news, Alice? I did not come here merely for pleasure, but to perform an important mission. Do not fear, Alice : it is joyful news, but so strange and so happy, I am afraid you will not bear it well. Are you quite strong, and ready to hear it?" she continued, looking earnestly into her face.

Alice never allowed emotion or surprise to rob her of her presence of mind. She sat still, trying to think what this sudden good news could be. She could think of nothing but Fred. Had he done something noble, and so brought credit upon them all? Or perhaps his industry and genius had been rewarded, and some hopeful future opened before him. As these simple and pleasing hopes appealed to her mind, she turned a brightening face towards Ellen, and gave her full assurance that she was fully able to listen to all she might relate. Little did she dream how much fortitude and strength it would require to hear it.

"It is a long story, dear Alice," began Ellen; "and you must not interrupt me. You know, Alice, my brother has been situated at Florence for two years. He has a studio there ; and his business brings him in contact with many travellers who visit the studios for pleasure, or to gratify their love of the beautiful in art. · These visitors come in and go out as they like ; while Charles continues his work, sometimes not noticing a single face that passes through his rooms.   One day, as he was at work copying a picture of Guido, he observed a tall, dark-looking gentleman taking a survey of the rooms, and looking at the pictures with an indifferent eye. Charles had finished not long before a portrait from memory of his sister and her friend Alice.   This picture hung in an obscure corner; for you know Charles has queer notions, and he had taken a fancy that this picture was too sacred for common eyes."

Ellen glanced at Alice.   She was looking at her intently, — a look half of doubt, half of wonderment; but Ellen saw that as yet she had no suspicion of the truth.

" The dark gentleman sauntered towards this corner, and carelessly turned the picture to the light. Charles says the portrait was called very good.   Mr. and Mrs. Cushing had seen it, and offered him a large sum for it; but he would not part with it. Your arm, dear Alice, was around my waist. Your lips were half parted, as if in girlish talk, and your eyes looked out from the canvas as they do on all your friends, with a tender light that seems to have something of sadness in it."

Alice moved impatiently.   " Your story is too romantic, Ellen, and you flatter a little too much."

" You were not to interrupt me, you know," said

Ellen. " Besides, Alice, I never can help being a little poetical. It is a failing of mine. Charles had taken great pains with my portrait. A wreath of blue violets was twined in my hair, which fell in long ringlets ; and one hand held up a white apron half filled with wild flowers. Altogether it was called a very pretty picture, though most persons supposed it a fancy sketch. As I have said, the stranger turned the picture to the light. For one moment he seemed spell-bound, bewildered. He pressed his hand to his forehead, and gazed long and earnestly at the picture ; while his cheeks and lips became of an ashy paleness, which even the dark skin could not conceal. With rapid strides he came to Charles's side ; and, while my brother sat with idle pencil, and in mute surprise, he gasped out, ' Mr. Lee, for the love of Heaven, tell me where you got that picture ! '

" ' It is my sister Ellen and a friend of her's,' " said he. ' It is not intended for the public eye. I painted it myself from memory.'

" The stranger's face betokened great agitation, and he trembled visibly. ' What is the name of the friend ? ' was the next question, — asked eagerly, and yet with a seeming dread of the answer.

" ' Alice Morton, sir,' said Charles, much wondering who the curious person could be.

" ' It is ! it is ! Can it be the child of my Mary, my own little Alice ? but no, — that were too great

11*

mercy,' he muttered in broken syllables, as he sank into a chair."

Ellen stopped in her story; for Alice had risen from her seat in eager expectancy, — every feature alive with feeling, her lips colorless, while her hands clutched the table nervously to keep from falling.

" Sit down, Alice," said Ellen, leading her forcibly to a seat. " This is too much for you. I might have known it. Why did I not wait till to-morrow? You are faint."

" No, no! " said Alice. " I am better I never faint. It is only a little weakness. But, Ellen, you are not trifling with me? You would not tell me all this for mere amusement. But it cannot be true. It is not! — is it? "

" It is all true," said Ellen. " But, my dear friend, l cannot go on till I see you better. Would it not be well to finish to-morrow? You will be stronger then."

" No, ·no! I *must* hear now. I *will*," said Alice eagerly. " Who was he? "

" At the gentleman's wish," continued Ellen, " my brother gave him your age and home, your character and past history. Alice, you must have guessed the truth. It was your father. He seemed bowed to the earth when Charles told him of your trials, your poverty. He seemed to be a man who had exhausted life, — who had been disappointed.

But he will find a lost treasure ; and you, Alice, will have a father."

"O my God!" said Alice, "is this you tell me true? Where has he been all these long years? Oh! why, why was my mother left to die without the knowledge that he, her best-beloved, was yet alive? Why was .I left to the crushing thought that I was an orphan and unloved? Oh! my father! my bitter childhood might have been spared me if I had been taken into your .loving arms. I have seen so much of life and the heart, Ellen, I can never be the confiding child I should have been had he been here to protect me."

Once Alice had stood with words of counsel and courage for Ellen. Now their places were reversed. Sympathy beamed from every feature of Ellen's face ; her arm stole softly around her friend's waist ; and the tears, which now would have their way, were kissed off by loving lips. "Remember, Alice, that we are made perfect through suffering. Heaven grant that your trials are ended, and that the future may be a constant peace, a heart-rest. You have been a loving and earnest worker.. I know that now you will have your reward. Your father has been for seven years in India. My brother informs me in his letter that he is reputed wealthy. I cannot tell you as your father would, so I will give you the packet he has forwarded."

CHAPTER XXIX

ALICE hardly knew how she reached her chamber. Her uncle's family had long since retired; but Alice had not thought of any thing save the packet in her hand, and the mysterious unfolding of human life and deep feeling she knew it must contain. There are times when some great sorrow or sudden joy so fills the depths of the soul, that its troubled waters must find vent in tears. Alice wept; and it was what she had long needed. Then, throwing herself upon her knees, she implored strength of that Father whose aid is ever present, to bear whatsoever might be in store for her, either of joy or sorrow.

A long curl of dark hair dropped from the packet, and wound about her fingers. It was her own. She remembered the very day her father had cut it from her head, when she sat upon his knee and listened in childish wonderment, while he told her he must go away a great many miles, and be absent a great many years. How true that prophecy had been! A picture of her mother was also there. She dropped a few tears over the beloved face, and then turned eagerly to read the closely written pages before her : —

My own dear and never-forgotten Alice,— How my heart yearns towards you, as the only hope I now have in life! My own little Alice,— can I believe that your eyes will see these lines; that your lips will once more speak that blessed word, "Father"? I have thought you dead, my child. I have mourned for you as one who was, and is not. Do not blame me, Alice, for neglect or forgetfulness. You will not, when I tell you how sad my life has been,— how many bitter days and nights I have passed in weariness. Be like your mother,— ever gentle, ever forgiving.

As briefly as possible I will tell you my story.

You were quite a child, Alice, when I left home. For two years I was gladdened with letters from friends in the East. My health was good, and my success as great as could be expected. Probably you know, my child, that I went to the mines. How often have I regretted it since! The severe labor and hard fare of a miner's life wore upon me at last. I was cheered by no kind sympathy from home. Fortune seemed to frown on every undertaking. My mournful fancy pictured my wife and child dying of want, or dependants on the rude charities of the world. Do you wonder, Alice, that fatigue and a twofold despair made me sick at last? For months I lay in a low fever, unsettled in mind and feeble in body, with no care save the rough though kindly nursing of the poor miners. The truest humanity is oftenest found among the uncultivated poor. I learned that then. Heaven be merciful to them, as they were to me!

No one thought that I could survive,— indeed, it was reported that I was dead. But, by little and little, my strength returned. I went back to life, bearing it but for one purpose, — to work for my family, or to hear some tidings of them.

Then came the crushing report that my wife and child were dead.

Frantic with the fear of losing every thing worth living for, I sent letter after letter to the East; but days, weeks, months passed, and still no tidings. What became of those letters, I

never knew. I do not think they ever reached their destination.
Probably they were opened for the money they contained; for
I denied myself every thing, — almost starved myself, — to send
each time some scanty pittance to those who, if yet living, I
would have died to save from one thought of privation. Reck-
less of every thing in my despair, I would have returned and
sought for you myself, and learn certainly if the terrible rumor
were indeed truth; but one day, as I was going to the city post-
office, — I did so now daily, having abandoned my mining labors,
— I met a friend from Connecticut, a native of our own dear
town. My heart leaped up with a sudden bound, and the question I most wished to ask, yet the answer to which I dreaded,
trembled on my tongue. The man started as if he had seen a
vision. " Your friends all think you dead," said he. " We
heard you had died of a fever." He told me that he had been
removed from Connecticut some time, — that my wife and child
were dead for a certainty; and he gave me the full particulars
of my poor Mary's last sickness. With regard to you, he was
not able to say when, where, or how you had died; but he said
he had received the information on good authority, and I believed him. I now no longer wondered that I received no letters from family or friends. They believed me dead. From
that day life was a blank to me. I no longer cared what became
of me. I could not go back to look at the graves of my wife
and child. What had I to do in a country that held only graves
for me? I shipped on board a merchantman for India. Afterwards, I learned that the person who informed me of your
death had been killed by the Indians in a skirmish. So you see
how all hope of your hearing of me was cut off; for I took no
pains to correct the impression of my death, preferring, since I
had died to happiness, to die to the world also. I courted
death in a thousand forms. I climbed to the highest mast in a
fierce storm, when the hearts of the stout sailors shrunk from
the duty. I saw the young and happy swept from me like
summer dew-drops; but death passed me, as he always does
the worn-out, waiting soul. Fortune turned her wheel favor-

ingly, now that I cared not for her favors. Wealth flowed in upon me; but I sat a dark, weary man, whose only peace was in spending his abundance in charity. I made the poor my family, told no one of my past history; and many wondered at the strange man, who seemed to carry a secret with him which the world could never know.

But sorrow and trouble and years began to tell their tales. My hair began to be sprinkled with gray. Though still a young man, my residence at the south had robbed me of my fresh vigor. I resolved to make a long tour of Europe; and then, if Heaven willed it, I would make a pilgrimage to my loved ones' graves, and die. It was while at Florence that I saw your portrait. It was the speaking picture of your mother in her girlhood, only a little sadder, — a little more tenderly thoughtful. O Alice! I might have prevented those shades on your face. Heaven forgive me!

And now, Alice, tenderly lov-d, will you not come to me, and let me love you, and repay you for all your past years of weariness and toil? God bless your uncle for his kind care of you! But oh, my child! have not the longing arms, the tender love, of a parent some claim upon your sympathy, even though they once let you slip from their embrace? I would come to you, but my health has never been good since my India life; and the excitement of this discovery has so wrought upon me, that my physicians utterly forbid my making the attempt. So will you not come to me for a season, and we will all return together? I have made friends of Mr. Cushing and his lady, and am now staying with them. Their arms are also open to receive you. Thank God that I have found a daughter, and that I have found one so true, so Christian-like, as your friends here report! Your friend, Ellen. Lee, her brother informs me, will reach here in the fall. I wish you to join her party. May God keep you in safety! Hope beckons us in the future, and Faith points us to rest at last.

Your loving father,
EDWARD MORTON.

There were other letters, explanatory and business.   Mr. Morton had placed abundant funds at
her disposal, and appointed for her a business agent
in New York.   Alice thought little of these.   She
only knew that a change so happy had come upon
her, that so blessed a protection was offered her, that
she seemed in a dream.   And then a feeling of
peace came over her, — of devout thankfulness ; and
she folded her hands together, and bowed her head,
as if a voice had said, " Let us pray."

CHAPTER XXX

THEY had all followed her down the garden walk, Nina and Freddy and Edward; and the judge stood holding back the gate for her to pass out.

"I suppose," said he, with the old twinkle in his eye, "that now our Miss Alice has grown so rich a lady, she will forget her humble friends, or put us down in the list of her poor relations."

Little Freddy clung to the skirt of her dress, and looked up wistfully into her face, as if he half comprehended he was going to part from a friend; while Nina seized her hand impulsively, and said, "What, Miss Alice grow proud! I don't believe she could; do you, Edward?"

The emphatic "No" which answered this seemed to satisfy all parties that it was simply impossible for Alice to be other than her own sweet self, money or no money: only the judge shook his head, and said something about its being unlawful to trust the evidence of a partial or interested person.

"How is your uncle, Alice?" said the judge. "Does he like the idea of parting with his *protégé?*"

"He is well," replied Alice; "but he says he should like to keep me a little longer."

"So we all should, indeed," was the reply. "I
hardly know what Nina will do without her 'good
model,' as she calls you. Ah! my dear girl," he
added in a changed voice, "you are richer in the
love of those innocent hearts you have been guiding,
than you will ever be in worldly goods. If I were
going across the sea, I should be sure to take passage with you; for the Father's eye will surely guard
well that dear one for whom so many pure prayers
rise daily."

Alice turned away to hide her emotion, and brush
away a few tears; she could not think of her approaching separation from her pupils without a
pang. Then, grasping the judge's hand, she said,
"Wherever I go, my dear friend, I shall never
forget your kindness; I shall never forget the sympathy which has always cheered me, the ready help
in trouble, and the warm welcome I always met in
this house."

She passed out into the road.

"You shall always have that here," said the
judge.

Little Freddy wondered what made papa's eyes
look so bright. The truth was, Judge Hall's tender
heart brought a shining mist into his eyes.

He turned away and strode up the avenue, *pooh-
ing* and *pshawing* all the way; but still the bright
mist gathered in his eyes, and some of it even rolled
down his cheeks in the form of a few tears.

"I did not know how much I loved that girl," said he to himself, as he shut the door of his library, and began talking to himself about the folly of an old man like him being so tender-hearted.

It was strange how Alice had placed herself in the centre of almost every heart. Even the judge had felt her influence.

"I never believed so completely in the power of personal influence," said Edward, as they walked down the old road, "as I do now. My dear Alice, you make me ashamed of myself. When I look at the amount of good you have done, with your few advantages, I feel how I have wasted my life. I have you to thank for that happier philosophy which first taught me that only in constant labor for others can we find our own true happiness. Now I know that only he fulfils life's mission who makes his power the means of good to humanity."

"You did not always think so," said Alice.

"No," said Edward. "I was content to be idle, because I had no faith. And, I blush to say it! I had a little pride too. The mass of the people seemed so low, so uncultivated, that it seemed useless to try to help them up,—a thankless task not worth one's trouble. Now I see how neither the day nor the hour bringeth forth the perfect good, but much work and much patient waiting. I am willing to work because it is duty, leaving the issue to the great Former of destiny. It is your influence and example that has wrought this, Alice."

" No, not wholly, if at all, Edward. Your own heart would not let you rest. You were unsatisfied with yourself. One so. noble, so generous, as you are, could not long have remained an idler in the great work-field our Father has given us. If I have helped you any, I am only too happy. I will not say I had no influence, for we should be just to ourselves. We all have an influence. He who in excess of false humility denies it wrongs himself, in that he does himself injustice, and his Maker, in that he denies He has given him a soul and a heart."

Edward looked at her in admiration. " How much wisdom there is in a good heart!" said he. " What all my study could not teach me, your pure instincts revealed to you. I am glad on one account that you will leave me for a time, Alice."

She looked up inquiringly.

" Yes," he said, " I am going to try to make myself worthy of you. Henceforth it shall never be said of me, 'This man put his hand to the plough, and looked back.' Into the world, into the thickest of her hurry, her folly, her sinfulness, I will go, with the sword of justice and the olive of peace. What influence I have shall be exerted. I will plead the cause of the poor and the oppressed. I will break the power of the wicked and the proud. I will open the prison doors for those who are

wrongfully bound. Farewell, Alice! May the Lord
keep you in safety! Pray for me, that I fail not,
that I no longer waste my manhood for that which
profiteth nothing."

He was gone; and Alice sat down on the wide
doorstep at the old kitchen door, and wept freely.
The stars were coming out in the sky, when she entered the house. She was going away, to be absent
many months, and every familiar object seemed dear
to her. She stood quite still in the doorway, watching Content, as she went on with her work. Then,
advancing to the table, she said, " Do you remember,
Content, that this is my last night at home? "

" 'Member it, Miss Alice? 'Pears like dis chile
berry sorry all day! There'll be jis nuffin 't all left
when you've gone; " and Content put on such a
dolorous expression, and mopped up her sable face
so vigorously with her apron, that Alice laughed in
spite of herself. She had been making a prodigious
noise among the kettles, to cover her emotions; but
now she laid down her dishcloth, and, sinking on
the bench, sobbed outright. Alice soothed and
comforted her; reminded her of the good Friend
who is always at hand and present with us; encouraged her so simply and lovingly, that the good
creature stopped her tears, and looked up into Alice's
face, as if expecting to see some heavenly grace and
beauty there, instead of the girlish though grave
and tender features of her young teacher.

"May de good Lord bress ye, honey! I'se one ting I prays for, and dat is, dat they'll let us both in at de same door of de kingdom. 'Pears like I must have ye there."

The tears were not yet dry upon Alice's face when she joined the family. They were all there, Mr. and Mrs. Whiting, Fred and the girls.

Alice would take her departure early in the morning to join her friends some miles beyond, and this evening was sacred to love's farewell. The judge's family, with their ever-refined delicacy, had taken their leave of her, that they might not break the home-circle, which they knew held Alice as one of its most strong and cherished links.

There were loving tones and looks and words for the departing one; they rejoiced in her good fortune; they regretted their own loss; and they proved their affection so effectually, that Alice hardly knew whether she was more pleased or sorry that she was going into the arms of a long-lost parent.

But this was only natural. The present is warm, sunny, heart-endeared; the past, and even the hopeful future, are as a tale that is told, a dream to be realized. No wonder Alice lingered long, when she knew tried hearts held her so lovingly!

Is there not a reward in a good life? Hear what Ellen Lee said, as they left their old home and former friends: "Alice, your influence has leavened my whole life. All that I am I owe to you. I would rather have your genius than any other,— the genius for making every one happy around you. It is the true genius, Alice, — the poetry of a true life, set to music."

We must leave them awhile floating out upon the sea towards sunny Italy. As they watched the edge of the horizon fade into the sky, Ellen gave a last farewell to her native home in these lines : —

" Oh ebbing tide, bear on
    Over the mystic sea !
The last dim speck of that land is gone
    Which held but graves for me.

Here on the solemn main,
    Between the future and past,
My soul may gather her strength again,
    And stand in her might at last.

Oh ebbing tide, bear on !
    Across our souls the waves
Are ebbing away from the sin they have borne :
    They leave it a land of graves, —

Graves where we buried the past,
    Along with the folly it bore ;
And, listening softly, heard at last
    The mandate, ' Sin no more.'

Oh, sailor at the helm,
    Look out o'er the mystic sea ! —
For our vessel's port is that distant realm
    Which lies in eternity, —

And say what watch are we in,
  How does the good ship steer :
The land-breeze blows from the coasts of sin,
  And the rapids of death are near.

Oh ebbing tide, bear on
  Over Life's ocean deep !
For our vessel is stout and our hearts are strong,
  And we've put our fears to sleep.

Over the mystic sea,
  Beyond the graves of sin,
The gates of heaven shall open to me,
  And God shall welcome me in.

Bear on, oh ebbing sea !
  Our sails to the winds are given ;
God is our Captain and Guide, and he
  Will pilot us all to heaven.

CHAPTER XXXI.

THE soft June sunlight fell as merrily, and the birds sang their matin hymns as sweetly, in the little village of Elmwood, as if five long years had not elapsed since we saw it last. Ah, reader! are you looking for the old Lee Farm? and do you expect to see our friends, the Whitings, still there? The Lee farmhouse still nestles amid its elms and maples; but Mr. Whiting has gone back to New York, and you must seek him in the same marble-fronted palace he occupied when our story opened.

But I have another scene for your eyes to-day. Look where the church-spire flashes in the morning rays. The dew is yet upon the grass, and the early freshness of the dawn lingers with the breath of flowers in every road and by-path. Still the villagers are astir. Groups of merry, laughing children might be seen almost running in the direction of the church. Knots of gay maidens and young men are scattered here and there, all in their holiday dress; for two of their most loved companions — and long absent too — are to be married to-day. It was the marriage of Alice which the villagers flocked to witness. One called to mind how good Miss Alice had been when her dear boy was sick;

12

and another, how beautifully she talked to her when she lay ill of a fever. And many blessed the noble Edward, who had stood, not with words only, but with hands full of comforts for his dear brothers in poverty.

A bridal procession swept down the aisle, and paused before the altar. The bride looked little different from our Alice of old, — only the promise of her girlhood has been realized in the tall, noble-looking woman; and her face, though still plain in repose, is marked with such a high expression, and speaks so much of soul, that the beholder, at first sight, would call her really beautiful. Such a charm, as of innocence and peace, seemed to float around her, that the villagers declared ever after that she was more of an angel than had stood at that altar for many a long year.

There is no nobler sight on all God's earth than a young, hopeful heart giving itself and its affections for life to another. Mr. and Mrs. Whiting both wept as Alice's clear responses rang out over the crowded house; and her father sobbed like a child during the whole service. The good old pastor, who had fed the Lord's lambs in that place for nearly half a century, placed his trembling hands on their heads as they knelt before him, and said, " May our Father love you and bless you, and give you the ' peace that passeth all understanding,' and keep you in his keeping! "

The judge had forgotten none of his old-fashioned hospitality. The doors of the "great house," as the villagers called it, were thrown open for a festival. Long tables were set on the green lawn, and music and dancing madè the blood leap with quicker bounds through every vein. Amidst it all, a family group sat in the library, and talked lovingly of the past and hopefully of the future. Alice's father had been received among them long ago, and now welcomed his son-in-law with even more than paternal fervor. "Remember, my children," he said, "that you are all I have; and try to love me a little. I am sad and grave, I know; but the shadow of a great sorrow is on my heart. Alice is a good girl, —just like her dead mother. May she prove the blessing to you that she was to me!"

"She has proved a blessing to all of us, and to all who ever knew her," said the judge, kissing her cheek. "It is all I wished to see, the two I loved best united;" and the judge rubbed his hands with intense satisfaction.

"Who would have thought," said Fred, "when Alice came to our house a poor orphan, that she would one day return to us more than we ever have given her, both in a moral and pecuniary sense? She formed my character. All that I am, or ever shall be, I owe to her."

"She saved me from the quicksands of folly and vanity," said Ada.

"And held up the glass to me," said Lizzie, "so that I saw my own deformity. I felt bitter towards her once ; now I repent, and wish her every happiness."

"My children," said Mr. Whiting, with moistening eyes, "God bless you all, and God bless the self-sacrificing girl who has made us all so happy! Heaven, in its wisdom, has seen fit to punish our pride, and exalt her humility. Never forget, my children, the true riches. We were never so poor, as amidst our so-called wealth."

Mrs. Whiting, now that she had become surrounded with her former atmosphere of wealth, had regained all her fashionable pride. She murmured as much as ever, though her heart seemed to have warmed somewhat towards her niece and children, when she saw their noble bearing in poverty. But she never ceased to regret that her daughters had acquired such vulgar tastes, and lost their relish for fashion and dress. "Alice was a very pretty bride," she said, "and her husband is one to be proud of; but I shall never forgive her for not being married in New York, and having a wedding-party."

Reader, if you will search among the many beautiful mansions which dot the banks of the Hudson, you will somewhere find the peaceful home of Edward Hall and his noble wife. Not in the rapid whirl of fashion is their pathway laid. When they married they entered into a solemn covenant to help one another in faith, in love, and in duty. Hand in hand they are passing along a sunny road, brightened by a love which is centred and bounded by the divine love; and the angels of Peace and Charity come and go over their threshold, and make them blessed. The harp, whose pure tones first taught Edward the melodies of truth, plays for him always; for Alice's heart is all his own, and his monitor still walks by his side with the words he loves to hear.

The judge's house in Elmwood is shut up, for he could not live apart from his son; and his arm-chair stands opposite the one where Alice's father sits. Only once a year they all go the "old place," and live over a past which had mingled with it much of pleasure as well as painful experience. Nina is now grown to be a tall young lady, and entertains her father's friends with dignified politeness; but after all I suspect she is something of a romp, for the broken limb of a cherry-tree in the orchard still testifies to the sad effect of her last feat at climbing. Little Freddy takes private lessons of Alice (for she has never quite outgrown the teacher), and shows his father long "sums," neatly copied on his slate. And the judge will look first at the slate, then at the rosy face of the boy, and back to the slate again; and finally, taking off his spectacles,

12*

he wipes them carefully with his silk handkerchief.
What do you suppose it is for?

We must not forget our old friend Sam. He is
no longer farm-boy ; but his ready wit and shrewd-
ness has advanced him to the post of chief overseer
on the estates of our friends at Elmwood. He has
never outgrown his talent for telling white lies, and
makes as queer speeches as ever. But, to this day,
the chief object of his veneration is Miss Alice.

Poor old Content has long since entered the kingdom which it was her chief delight to anticipate in
life. Alice shed as many tears over her old friend
as if she had been heiress of untold wealth, and
firmly believes that she shall see her in heaven,
and hold her.

Of Mr. Whiting's family much might be said ;
and yet a little will sum up all. Fred has received
a splendid education, and plead his first cause. It
was a brilliant triumph, and placed him at once in
the full blaze of the public eye. Edward Hall
watches over him, anxious lest the too great flat-
teries of his admirers should lead him astray from
that centre of duty which alone should be the principle of a true and noble life. Everywhere Edward
Hall's name is spoken with respect. First and
foremost in the cause of the weak, earnest and
truthful though the world should frown, — there are
many honest tongues ready to praise him, and many
hearts which remember him in their prayers. He

is rich, and does not need to labor; but he seeks out the poor and oppressed, and rights them by the thunder of his eloquence, or the still voice of his all-subduing humanity.

Lizzie and Ada still remain at home; proving by quiet ministrations how much they are changed from the selfish, vain girls we once knew them. They make their father's life truly a blessed one. The heavy curtains no longer shut out the sunlight from the rooms; but every thing bright and beautiful finds a home there. And every Christmas Eve a family party gathers there; and old-fashioned simplicity makes their hearts young and fresh as a May morning.

Mr. and Mrs. Cushing resides on the banks of the Hudson, not far from Alice's home. They have at last adopted her into their love; and Alice calls Mrs. Cushing "mother," as she promised she would perhaps do some day. Happy Alice, to be so loved by many hearts!

Charles and Ellen Lee have been at home a month. Charles is now a painter of some celebrity; but perhaps no picture which he ever executed has brought him so many blessings as the portraits of Ellen and Alice. When Alice was married, he made her a present of it, and it now hangs in the library; and Mr. Morton never passes it without a sad look and tearful eyes. Ellen has indeed made her genius the means of good to others. Many good and valuable books testify to the labor of her pen; and many foreign friends will long remember the young American poetess. And there is a rumor that Fred admires and loves the reflection of his dear Alice as he sees it in Ellen, and that she will soon be Mrs. Frederick Whiting. As for Charles, he is wedded to his art.

There is one more of whom I fain would speak. Ellen Lee is a large-hearted, benevolent woman, and often pursues her missions of charity through the crowded lanes of New York. One day a note was brought her from a dying woman, praying her assistance. She went immediately. Judge of her surprise to find, in the emaciated and friendless being before her, her once cruel enemy, Evelina Cobb. Tenderly she nursed and soothed her. The poor woman was nervous, and told Ellen, with tears and protestations of grief, how much she repented of her former wickedness. "I believe," she said, "that God has sent these sorrows upon me for my youthful sins. I am dying; so I may ask you to forgive me." Ellen wept and prayed over her, and listened in sad pity, while she told her that her husband's name was Eugene Lovering, and that he was in the State Prison, sentenced for many years. Her only child had died from want of proper food and care. It truly seemed like a judgment. The noble woman she had so wronged stood before her like an angel of mercy, — nursed her, comforted her, prayed for her, and at last brought her back to life, and found her a home and friends. "The last shall be first, and the first last."

Lizzie especially interested herself for her. The great lesson of her life had been taught her by the man who was the cause of all this misery. But Evelina never was aware that Lizzie Whiting had known her degraded husband. Eugene Lovering, she said, had beguiled her by flattering words and great promises; and she, having no basis of principle, left her father's house, and they cast her off for ever. She had been married in a Roman Catholic Chapel.

It was strange that it had not occurred to Alice before that the writer of that note might be Evelina Cobb.

"There is that maketh himself rich, yet hath nothing." The love of money and the foolish vanities of the world had proved Mr. Whiting's ruin. Then he shut his soul up to the pleadings of conscience, — till a voice which he had learned to love stole in soft accents to his ear; till the hand of a child had led him into the low valleys of Peace; and the example of a daily life, whose very atmosphere was goodness, taught him wisdom, and made him a better man. Through the aid of Alice's father, he regained his former wealth; but in the large library you will find one improvement. This is a marble tablet, on which is inscribed, in letters of gold, this scripture text: "Let not the rich man glory in his riches; but let him that glorieth glory in this, — that he understandeth and knoweth me; that I am the Lord, which exercise loving kindness, judgment, and righteousness in the earth."

To Alice the promise is fulfilled at last. She went forth a noble and earnest laborer. She sowed in tears; now she reaps in joy. Her whole life is like a harvest-day, bright with sunny gleamings, filled with song and gladness. Yes, from the field of labor she returned homeward with singing and thanksgiving, bearing her precious "Sheaves" with her.

THE END.

www.ingramcontent.com/pod-product-compliance
Lightning Source LLC
Chambersburg PA
CBHW021050030726

47496CB00006B/1778